MW00893972

414
FIC
TWO

DEC 2 3 2003

Beachmont
Letters

Also by Cathleen Twomey

Charlotte's Choice

Beachmont Letters

Cathleen Twomey

Boyds Mills Press

Published by Boyds Mills Press, Inc.
A Highlights Company
815 Church Street
Honesdale, Pennsylvania 18431
Printed in China

Publisher Cataloging-in-Publication Data (U.S)

Twomey, Cathleen.
     Beachmont letters / by Cathleen Twomey. — 1st ed.
[256] p. ;   cm.
Summary: Scarred by a fire that killed her father, a seventeen-year-old
girl begins a correspondence with a young soldier in 1944.
ISBN 1-59078-050-7
1. Fire —Psychological aspects — Fiction — Juvenile literature. 2. Fathers
and daughters — Fiction — Juvenile literature.   I. Title.
    [F] 21   2003
2002111301

First edition, 2003
The text of this book is set in 12.5-point Times New Roman.
Edited by Greg Linder

Visit our Web site at
www.boydsmillspress.com

10 9 8 7 6 5 4 3 2 1

Acknowledgments

My heartfelt thanks to the following people:

My father, Edward J. Twomey—for listening, even when all I have
to give is silence.

Peg Derrivan Purington—for a lifetime of friendship, laughter,
and dreams.

Susi and Liza Richardson and Nancy Carberry Barthelemy—for
your advice and support.

Kent Brown Jr.—for keeping me writing and keeping me
from worrying.

The Vermont College Writing for Children staff, students,
and faculty, especially Marion Dane Bauer, Jane Resh
Thomas, Norma Fox Mazer, and Louise Hawes—for the
gift not only of knowledge, but also of yourselves.

"The Cave," including Suzanne Byrnes, Lisa Dougher, Karen
Fisher-Baird, Wilmoth Foreman, Wendy Herumin, Maurene
Hinds, Amy Shires, Pat Snodgrass, Wendy Townshend,
Jeremy Wailes, and Beckie Weinheimer—for teaching me
that home is wherever love resides.

Pat Linder—for sharing your family, your home, and those
beautiful Wisconsin dragonflies.

Iris and Guthrie Linder—for helping me to discover magic
in the simplest moments of life.

Bear Writers, Fran Hodgkins, and the Saugus Children's
Writers Group, Katy Carlin, Edward J. Twomey, Jr., Mary C.
Twomey, Fred Bailey, Carol Frizzell, and Judy Crawford.

The children at Shriner's Hospital in Boston.

Chapter One

❧ ❧

Five houses until Mr. Partenope reached the Carvellis'
house. One hundred ninety-three steps in all. Eleanor had
counted each one. Every morning except Sunday, and
weekday afternoons at two, she stood on the bottom step of
Mr. and Mrs. Carvelli's two-family house. She waited while
Mr. Partenope trudged along, dropping mail into the front-
door slots of every house on Everett Street. She bounced a
little on her heels while she waited, as if she were seven —
her sister Lindy's age — and not seventeen. But bouncing
and counting along with each of Mr. Partenope's steps didn't
make the waiting any easier. No one on earth walked as
slowly as Mr. Partenope did. Babies just learning to put one
foot in front of the other didn't walk that slowly.

"How you doing, Eleanor?" he called from the Sullivans'
front stoop. "Cool enough for you? Frost was on the pumpkin
last night, I'm telling you." He looked both ways before he
crossed the street, then looked again. "Beginning of June,

and the wife wanted to turn up the heat. I like it this way, though. Doesn't take me as long to walk the old route. Know what I mean?" Eleanor's fingers curled into her palms. She knew exactly what he meant. She also knew that if Mr. Partenope didn't talk to every blessed creature on the street, including the nonhuman ones, walking the route would never take him so long.

Of course, he hadn't been this chatty two weeks ago, at least not to her. On that afternoon, he stopped to greet the collie that lived in the corner house. The dog wriggled and squirmed and then wrapped its chain around Mr. Partenope's legs. *Whoosh!* Man and dog went down on the pavement with a definite crack that made Eleanor's own head ache. The mailbag flew out of his hands, scattering envelopes and magazines all over the street. Eleanor hurried to his side. "Are you all right?"

The corners of the mailman's mouth had already begun to curve into a grateful smile when his eyes found her face. They flicked across it once, then darted away. His lips closed over the gap between his front teeth and tightened into a line. The whole time Eleanor was untangling the dog and bending down to retrieve the envelopes and newspapers that looked like pieces of a giant puzzle strewn across the road, he had examined each envelope, had refolded each newspaper and each magazine.

"Thank you," Mr. Partenope said finally when Eleanor had gathered all the mail into a neat pile beside him. But he didn't look at her face. Instead, his gaze jumped from earth to sky to somewhere in the middle of Eleanor's stomach. And except for that thank you, he hadn't said another word.

These days Mr. Partenope's eyes still jumped from earth

to sky to somewhere in the middle of Eleanor's stomach, but he certainly didn't have any more trouble talking. "Just might have something for you, young lady," he announced. He stood leaning against Carvellis' front gate and inspected the envelopes in his hand. It hurt—the way he avoided looking at her. Maybe not like skinning a knee or cracking an ankle against the bed in the middle of the night, but deep inside, in Eleanor's stomach, and even her lungs.

"You said you had mail?" she asked.

Mr. Partenope's breath came in little spurts. "Honey, I always have mail." He chuckled as he handed her the pile of envelopes. "Mind you now, the bottom bunch is for the Carvellis. Bottom of the pile, bottom apartment. See? I got a system. I shouldn't really be giving their mail to you. Regulations, you know. But these old dogs . . ." He looked at his feet. "They are getting plumb worn out these days. Flat feet, army says. Can't use someone with flat feet. Flat feet, my foot. It's all right to give me a route and a half on weekdays, though."

Mr. Partenope should have married Mrs. Carvelli. Eleanor had a brief picture of them talking each other to death over breakfast.

Eleanor's toes tapped against the inside of her shoe. "Thank you very much, Mr. Partenope." She hugged the mail to her chest.

Mr. Partenope cleared his throat. "Best be getting on. Lots of letters these days. People writing more and more." But his feet stayed exactly where they were, as if they were made of cement, as if no power on earth could move them.

Eleanor's mouth ached from smiling too much. "It's just one of those things," she said. "I'm sure people appreciate seeing you hurrying down the street with their mail."

"Well, I suppose," Mr. Partenope said. He saluted Eleanor with his right hand. Then he turned and headed toward the Beauchamps' triple-decker next door.

Seventeen steps until he reached their door. Seventy-three until he turned the corner onto Fowler Street. Eleanor had counted every one of those steps, too. Seventy-three steps more and she could search through the pile of envelopes. Ten steps farther. Nine. Eight . . .

Her fingers shuffled the letters. Bill, bill, bill. *Bingo!* Fourth from the top, she found it—the red-and-blue-bordered envelope with her name and address on it: Eleanor P. Driscoll, 13 Everett Street, Beachmont, Massachusetts. She touched the "E" in Eleanor. Black and bold, the letter reminded her of the way Daddy used to print "To Eleanor P. Driscoll" on the envelopes of all her birthday cards. As if she meant more to him than just plain Eleanor.

She pushed the memory out of her mind and concentrated on the name on the envelope instead: *Cpl. Robert Bettencourt.* The rest of the mail she dropped into the slot in the Carvellis' front door. Then she was off, down the steps two at a time and onto the sidewalk. Her fingers traced the edge of the envelope as she walked. *Robert, Robert, Robert.* The man at the end of the street trimming his tiny patch of lawn looked up. When his eyes touched hers, he suddenly became preoccupied with the handle of his shears. He always did that — as if the sight of Eleanor would strike him dead.

Eleanor usually stared right at him, willing him to look up. But not today. Today the man could hide his eyes. He could spend the rest of his life inspecting his trimmers. Because Eleanor didn't care. Not this morning. *Robert, Robert, Robert.* Each syllable was a beat in her song. She added *beach, beach, beach* when she crossed from Everett Street to Ocean Avenue. Some things just went together, like brownies and milk, like Abbott and Costello.

Like Robert's letter and the ocean.

Eleanor climbed right out onto the sea wall and let her legs hang over the edge. She breathed deeply, allowing the vinegary ocean smell fill her. Thank God for cold afternoons in this place. She had no people storms to hide from today. No children crawled over the rocks to play tag at the water's edge. No bigger boys armed with pebbles played War out by the pier.

People might not bring down trees or power lines like wind and snow did, but they certainly brought her down. The way they acted when they saw her ground away pieces of her, just like the waves ground away stones until there was nothing left but sand.

Eleanor's fingers itched to take the letter out of her pocket, but she had to check for intruders just one last time — behind the beach roses, and across the cliffs to the sand below where gulls scavenged along the shore, complaining to each other in crabby old lady voices. *Safe.* Today Mahoney's Point belonged to her alone.

Her and Robert. She pulled out the red-and-blue-bordered envelope and tore open its flap.

The letter was written in pencil on sheets of tissue-thin

paper. She read it three times. The first time, she gulped the words down as if she were downing a glass of lemonade on a scorching afternoon. The next time, she read each word out loud. A gull, perched on the wall beside her, blinked his eyes, and she pretended she was reading the letter to the bird. *Dear Eleanor, please don't apologize for anything you write . . .*

The third time Eleanor read Robert's words, she savored each one, tasting the sounds as they rolled off her tongue.

June 8, 1944

Dear Eleanor,

Please don't apologize for anything you write. I enjoy your letters. I enjoy the way you tell stories, the way you describe people. I can see your mother, your sister Lindy, and your neighbor Mrs. Carvelli as if they were standing right in front of me. Your letters sound the way I imagine you — warm and bright and funny.

Things are pretty quiet around the campus, in spite of the invasion. We go to class and learn four-letter words in French and German. Sorry, but it's true. The army, in its infinite wisdom, thinks we should know when someone is swearing at us in another language.

The other guys call us ASTP forces the "All Safe 'Til Peace" squad. My buddy Tom O'Connor says, "Don't let it bother you, Robert." But it does. Eleanor, the only reason I'm here is because I flunked Greek and had to take an extra year of French. So I get to be a translator. It doesn't seem fair somehow. The guys I went to school with, the guys who studied their hearts out, are getting shot up in the Pacific or crawling over a beach in France.

It's fate, I suppose. I think a lot about fate these days. What if your English teacher — Sister Agnes, was it? — hadn't given you the assignment of writing to a soldier? What if I hadn't gone to mail call that day?

I'm very glad I'm the one who received your letter, Eleanor. Take care of yourself.

Affectionately,
Robert

Affectionately. Eleanor pressed Robert's letter to her cheek and squeezed her eyes shut. Not "Sincerely yours" or "Very truly yours," the way he had signed every other letter. She stretched her legs out in front of her. Her toes wriggled in the air, as if she were tap-dancing across the beach in bare feet. A thousand screaming children could have invaded the beach now and she wouldn't have cared. They could attack, they could crawl all over the rocks and pelt her with beach roses. She had *Affectionately* to protect her.

Eleanor's toes stopped their dance. Robert's letter dropped to her lap. With the tips of her fingers, she touched her cheek, her chin, her neck. What an idiot she was. What a complete and total idiot! Robert didn't know about her face. If he did, he never would have signed his letter *Affectionately.*

The way Mrs. Carvelli blabbed everything to everyone, Robert was probably the only person in the entire universe who hadn't heard about "that poor scarred girl." Eleanor could still hear the woman's voice the Friday before last, when Eleanor and Lindy and Mama were moving into the apartment upstairs.

"*Sheesh.* I never saw so many books," Mrs. Carvelli had said, partly to Eleanor and partly to the moving men, who stopped after the twentieth box to down whole bottles of Coca-Cola in single gulps.

Eleanor sighed. She had been explaining things all afternoon to Mrs. Carvelli — why Daddy had a marble bust of Hippocrates, why he owned a black leather bag. "I told you. My father was a doctor. He had lots of medical books," she said.

Mrs. Carvelli shook her head from side to side. "Too bad he died in the fire, huh, Eleanor? 'Cause those other doctors, they don't fix you up so good."

Eleanor touched her cheek again. Her fingers traced the map of scars that ran from below her right eye down to her mouth and chin and neck. Melted wax, that's what her scars felt like. When she was little, she used to play with the wax that dripped from the candles Mama lit for dinner. Eleanor would warm the pieces in her hand until they were soft enough to spread across her palm.

Now she wore that melted wax on her face, for everyone to see, for everyone to avoid. Like Mr. Partenope. And the man in the corner house. *I want you to know, Mr. Partenope, and you, too, Man in the Corner House. There's a person underneath all these scars. Somebody who is "warm and bright and funny" and a whole lot of other things, too.* Things even Robert didn't know about. Like she had a bit of a temper. And a trace of stubbornness, too — inherited from

16

Mama, everyone said. Not that Eleanor wanted Robert to see that side of her. Not yet, anyway. Just like he didn't need to know about her face — yet — or the Palm Gardens fire — yet.

Or about Daddy. Eleanor tried not to think about him, tried not to remember Daddy's smile and his deep voice. But every time she closed her eyes, she saw him again at the restaurant, sitting across the table from her, wearing his tuxedo with the red boutonnière. *Ah, Eleanor. Sixteen years old and so grown up. You're not Daddy's little girl anymore. Except maybe just this one last time.*

"Ellie Belly, Mama said to come to supper now." Lindy stood on the edge of the sea wall, her hands resting on her hips. "I called you three times already."

"I'll be there in a minute." Eleanor tried sliding Robert's letter and its envelope into her pocket without her sister noticing. She should have known better. Lindy's mind-everyone-else's-business nose never missed a thing.

"What have you got?"

"Nothing!"

"Yes, you do. I saw. It's a letter. You got a letter from that boy."

"He's not a boy, Lindy. He's a college graduate."

"But you always read me the letters." Lindy's voice had that little kid whine to it that scraped across Eleanor's nerves.

"Later, maybe. What are we having for supper, anyway?"

"Tuna-pea wiggle," Lindy said. She scrunched her whole face together, as if she were watching someone clean a fish.

"That sounds disgusting."

"It smells that way, too. Mrs. Carvelli wanted to give

Mama some kind of red stuff instead, but Mama said maybe some other time. Will you read the letter to me at supper?"

Eleanor had an awful thought. "You didn't tell Mrs. Carvelli, did you? About Robert? You promised you wouldn't, remember?"

Lindy was indignant. "I didn't say anything to anyone! I don't tell secrets. I'm not a baby."

"You're seven years old, I know."

"So you'll read me Robert's letter? While we're eating?"

Hardly. Not with Mama sitting right across the table from her, listening to every word. "Maybe afterward." Eleanor caught one of Lindy's hands. "We'd better get going before Mama thinks we fell into the water and floated away with the tide."

"Do you think fish eat people-pea wiggle?" Lindy asked.

"Not if Mama cooks it."

Tuna-pea wiggle smelled as awful as Lindy had said it did. Eleanor tried poking at the stuff, but her stomach turned every time the lumpy mess plopped between the tines of her fork.

"I can't eat this," Mama said. She sat at the table with her elbows leaning on the edge, her hair frizzled into little curls around her face. "I'll be stopping by Bailey's Market tomorrow," she said. "Maybe you can make a list of things you want."

"Something edible," Eleanor said.

"Something not tunafish or Spam," Lindy agreed.

Mama scrunched her face exactly the way Lindy had.

"Thank God I'm a better nurse than I am a cook."

Lindy chattered away in her squeaky voice. "Mrs. Carvelli likes to cook. She has lots of pans and everything. She's going to make cookies for me someday soon."

Mrs. Carvelli had the time to do all the things Mama couldn't. She braided Lindy's hair, she crocheted tiny doll sweaters. Mama used to have time to make up stories and sing silly songs. But that was before Daddy died. "Mrs. Carvelli said I should come downstairs Sunday after she gets home from church, and she'll show me how to make raviolis," Lindy announced.

"She's very nice," Mama said. Her tone didn't sound as if she thought Mrs. Carvelli was very nice. She sounded as if she felt the way Eleanor did — that Angela Carvelli was too rude for words. But Mama was too polite to say so.

Suddenly, Mama let out a sigh. "Maybe you'll show Eleanor and me sometime." She reached over and tugged at one of Lindy's pigtails. "I'm going into the living room and just collapse for a while." She shuffled out of the room as if she were at least a hundred years old. Her voice even had that old person quiver to it when she paused in the doorway and called back, "I suppose we really should unpack those boxes in the back hall, but I just can't get myself in gear for it."

Neither could Eleanor. She had books and writing paper in those boxes, buried under the layers of Haviland china. But things didn't fit here the way they had in the old house. The apartment's rooms were tiny, and the place felt stiff and uncomfortable, like wet shoes that hadn't dried properly. Besides, without the built-in shelves they had in their other house, she would have to pile her books in the corner of the bedroom and tuck her writing paper into the bureau she and Lindy shared. Lindy's dolls took up every other inch of space in their room.

"That's what you need to do after we finish the dishes, Lindy," Eleanor said. "Find someplace else for your dolls."

Lindy bristled. Lindy's dolls were sacred. "You're not my boss."

"It's my room, too, and I need to be able to walk in there without breaking my neck."

Lindy's face collapsed. "You promised you'd show me the letter. The one from Robert."

"After you put your dolls away."

"Mama didn't say I had to."

"Mama's tired, Lindy. She's been working so hard. We have to be her helpers. That's all," Eleanor tried to explain, but Lindy was already stomping toward the bedroom.

It was easy to forget, sometimes, how young her sister really was.

Maybe later, when Eleanor was finished cleaning the kitchen, she would make it up to Lindy. Maybe she would find the Chinese checkerboard or read Robert's words out loud, so Lindy could sparkle the way she always did when he mentioned her name.

But Lindy fell asleep while Eleanor was reading Robert's letter to her. She lay curled on her bed, her arms wrapped around Cinderella, her blonde curls tangling with the doll's yellow hair on the pillow. Eleanor turned off the bedroom light and listened to the sound of Lindy's breathing, the click of her tongue against the roof of her mouth. *Of course* Lindy could sleep. Little kids could do that. They lived in a fantasy world, where people storms and money troubles and *Affectionately* didn't exist.

Sometimes Eleanor sat on the bed and wished so hard — wished until her skin hurt. She didn't even know what she was wishing for. Daddy? To have her old face back again? That someone somewhere would somehow make things better?

Mama looked so beaten and gray these days. Every evening after supper, she put her feet up on the hassock in the living room, and most nights she fell asleep before Lindy and Eleanor finished the dishes. If only Eleanor could help out more — earn some money, so Mama wouldn't have to work so many hours.

And what would she do about Robert? She had placed his letter in the shoebox under her bed with his other letters. She would have to write back soon, or he would worry the way she did sometimes, whether he had been too friendly, revealed too much of his true self. If she could just find the right words, so he would write *Affectionately* at the end of his next letter, too.

From the bedroom window, she watched men and women together on the sidewalk below. Some couples laughed and argued and leaned into each other as they walked along; some walked in silence, holding each other at arm's length. They were all heading toward Beachmont Park, to the dance halls and arcades and the tiny shacks that sold fried clams and onion rings. Whenever the breeze blew the curtain back from her open window, she smelled hot oil from the fryers. But Eleanor wasn't hungry anymore.

Those girls with their perfect faces and perfect lives, did

they realize how lucky they were? She had been one of those girls once. Jack Carmody tried to steal a kiss after the Winter Cotillion, and she'd let him. When she confessed her sin to Father Berube, he gave her a whole rosary to say for penance. Eleanor had wanted to spit, she was so angry. Fifty Hail Marys and ten Our Fathers for one little kiss? But tonight, she would say a million rosaries if only she could confess a sin like that just one more time.

With her fingernails, Eleanor pressed the skin on her cheek until she felt needles of pain through the scarring. What if a boy like Jack Carmody never wanted to take her to a dance again? What if she never again got to confess stolen kisses? What if in the whole rest of her life, she never ever had the chance to step off of a streetcar with some boy and walk, arm in arm with him, toward the music?

Eleanor crept out of bed and tiptoed into the kitchen. In the table drawer, she found Daddy's fountain pen and a pad of notepaper.

June 10, 1944

Dear Robert,

Thank you for liking my letters. Sometimes I feel as if I go on and on about nothing very interesting. I'm glad you enjoy them anyway.

The way the newspapers talk these days, maybe you'll never have to go overseas at all. Maybe you'll stay right in New York the whole time. You shouldn't feel guilty, though. My father used to say, "Everyone has his own part to play in this world." Being in New York right now is your part.

My mother has been working as a nurse at the Veteran's Hospital in Chelsea ever since Daddy died. That's what I always wanted to be — a nurse. At this rate, though, I'll be lucky if they don't put me in jail for murder first. I don't mind watching Lindy so much, but every time we set foot outside the house, Angela Carvelli makes a comment. "You shouldn't be letting your sister sit outside in the sun like that. She'll get heat stroke and drop right down dead," she tells me. Or, "Cold drinks on a warm stomach make for a sick child."

Mama says Mrs. Carvelli means well. And I know she does. But some days I just want to strangle the woman. If you don't hear from me for a while, you'll know what happened. Do you think the law takes excruciating circumstances into account? (That is a joke!)

I really do have to go. It's late and Lindy will be up with the sun, wanting to play dolls. I get to be her personal lady-in-waiting.

Please stay safe!

Affectionately,

Eleanor

P.S. I'm very glad you're the one who received my letter, too.

Chapter Two

❧ ❧

"**I**f I have to hear one more word about how perfect the world would be with Angela Carvelli running it, I am going to scream," Eleanor announced at breakfast. "Every minute of every day for the past two weeks, all she does is go on and on about how she would raise a daughter if she had one."

Mama placed her nursing cap into a shoebox. "Shhh. Not so loud. You'll wake Lindy," she said. "And it's Mrs. Carvelli, not Angela." Her voice softened. "Sweetie, try to be nice."

"You don't have to listen to that woman all day long, Mama. Wait until you hear what she says about women who work."

But Mama wasn't paying attention. She was too busy counting out change from the yellow-and-blue-flowered teapot onto the table. "Sweetie, I'd love to sit and talk some more, but I have to run. The streetcar has been early every day this week, and I can't afford to be late for work." She kissed Eleanor's cheek good-bye.

Eleanor sat at the table and read whatever sections remained from yesterday's *Globe*. But she couldn't concentrate. Her eyes kept returning to the teapot. In the house in Cape Ann, it had sat on a shelf above the kitchen window, beside pots of geraniums. Sometimes the teapot held daisies, or dandelions that Lindy picked for Mama. It never held money, at least not while Daddy was alive.

Eleanor turned the teapot over and emptied the change onto the table. One dollar and seventy-three cents. That was all. Not enough to buy new shoes for Lindy, now that her feet had outgrown every other pair. Not enough to pay even one of the bills stacked on the front hall table. Daddy had been so understanding with his patients, letting them pay whenever they could. After he died, everyone commented on his generosity. But compliments didn't pay those bills.

It wasn't Daddy's fault that there was no money. Eleanor dropped the change back into the teapot. But it wasn't Mama's fault, either, and she was the one having to worry about money now. Why couldn't somebody help Mama the way Daddy helped his patients?

Why couldn't *she* help? Eleanor rolled the thought over in her mind. She could find a job. She could work nights, weekends, maybe a couple of days, too. Then there would be two people earning money, not one. Mama could work less and spend a little time with Lindy, at least until fall when school started.

There were plenty of jobs around. The General Electric plant in Lynn was always advertising for help. She could do that. She could get a job. And the teapot would fill with dollar bills, not just coins. G.E. paid well for a factory job. That's what everybody said.

Lindy marched into the kitchen. She plunked herself down at the table and placed her doll on the chair next to her. "Cinderella needs an egg, mushed up, the way Mama makes them," Lindy demanded.

"Mama's not here, Lindy. And besides, you know you can't have eggs every day anymore. They're expensive, and the soldiers need them, remember?"

"I don't care about soldiers." Lindy's eyes filled with tears. "I don't care about anything. I want Mommy here, the way she used to be."

Eleanor wanted Mama here, too. She'd know what to do about Lindy's tears. They came too often lately, with that tremble in her voice and chin. "Hurry up and eat your cereal," she told Lindy. "When you're finished, I have a secret to tell you."

"Is it about Robert?"

"No, it's not about Robert. But I'm not telling you anything else until you finish eating."

Lindy shoveled spoonfuls of corn flakes into her mouth. Then she put the bowl to her lips and swallowed the milk in three gulps. "I'm done," she announced. "Tell me the secret now!"

"After you put your dish in the sink."

"You're awful bossy, you know that, Ellie Belly?" Lindy

dropped the bowl in the sink and followed Eleanor into the bedroom. "Now?"

"I'm going to look for a job. Maybe in one of those factories like the G.E. To help Mama pay the bills. Then she won't be so tired all the time."

Lindy danced around Eleanor, making it impossible for Eleanor to change her clothes. "And Mama will stay home? Do stuff with me?"

"Not all the time — and not at all if you don't scoot out of my way," Eleanor said, reaching around Lindy to grab her blouse and gingham jumper from the closet. "Now get out of here. I have to get dressed."

"Maybe Mama can play dolls with me the way she used to." Lindy inspected herself in the mirror hanging on the wall beside the closet, turning first one way and then the other.

Eleanor's stomach twisted. "Lindy, that's enough!" She covered the mirror with her bathrobe. "I'll never find a job if you don't let me get into my clothes. I need to be there when the office opens, and I still have to catch the streetcar and walk ten blocks across town."

Lindy's smile turned upside down, but only for a moment. "You'll have a real job in a real factory."

"Maybe. If I ever get there. Now go." Eleanor closed the door behind Lindy. Her fingers trembled so violently that the buttons on her blouse and jumper kept slipping through her fingers. *You can do this, Eleanor. You'll be fine. It's a factory. People will get used to the way you look. And if they don't, maybe they can put you someplace where people can't see you.* She reached for the bathrobe. Her hands squeezed the rough fabric, bunching it up until she could just see the reflection of her neck with its puckery skin that disappeared beneath her collar.

In the hospital, Dr. Gilligan had warned her before he removed her bandages. "You won't look like the old you," he said. Eleanor had hurried to the mirror, anyway.

"I'm almost pretty," Eleanor used to think, shaking her head slowly, letting her red hair swing softly against her shoulders. "I have pretty hair. Not strawberry red, like some people have, but a nice red. And nice skin, too.

Marybeth had agreed. "You have great bone structure, too. They look for that in movie stars, you know."

But that was before the fire.

Now in the hospital's mirror, Eleanor didn't see nice skin or great bone structure. She saw a phantom — a grotesque creature with a gash for a mouth and a melted-wax cheek and chin.

Where had the phantom come from? Eleanor checked behind her. No phantom there. She turned toward the mirror again and shook her head slowly from side to side. The phantom imitated her, swinging its red hair against cotton-covered shoulders. With trembling fingers, Eleanor touched the phantom's reflection. She pushed against the awful face. Then she pounded it with her fists.

The glass shattered into a hundred shards. When Eleanor bent down to pick them up, the phantom she had become stared back at her from every one of the pieces.

"Eleanor, it's all right," Dr. Gilligan said in a strained voice. "Someone else will do that. I don't want you to get hurt."

Hurt. Eleanor's hands dropped to the bureau. She picked up Mama's tortoiseshell brush and pulled it through her hair. Then she went straight to the shoebox and took out Robert's most recent letter. *Warm and bright and funny.* Maybe she could be that way. For today. She could pretend she wasn't wearing a phantom face, so Mama could stop worrying about money.

Knocking on the Carvellis' back door made Eleanor's teeth rattle. She had to keep reminding herself. *This is for Mama and Lindy.* They'd better appreciate it, too, because asking Mrs. Carvelli to watch Lindy while Eleanor was job hunting just about gave Eleanor hives.

Mrs. Carvelli had stuffed her round body into a pink housedress with embroidered cherries on each pocket, and she smiled as if she had solved the problems of the whole world. She didn't even wait for Eleanor to say good morning.

"Why, it's gotta be like one of those psychotic things. I mean, just this morning, Chubbs and me, we was just talking about you and your poor Mama. It's a sad thing, a woman losing her husband like that. And it's happening all over the place. Why, just last week, my sister's best friend's niece got one of those telegrams."

Eleanor had checked. G.E.'s employment office opened at nine. The way Mrs. Carvelli kept on talking, Eleanor would be lucky to arrive by noon. "Mrs. Carvelli, I need to ask you for a favor." Her voice wavered on the word *favor.*

"Why, sure. What d'you want, Eleanor? You want to borrow something? Cup of sugar, maybe?"

"I need you to watch Lindy for a couple of hours, if you wouldn't mind."

"You going out someplace? You need something? I can get my Chubbs to pick it up at his store. Then you don't have to go out."

"It's not that. It's just . . ." Eleanor's throat tightened.

Mrs. Carvelli jabbered away. "Like I says to Chubbs, 'We gotta do something for that woman and her girls. Being thrown out of their big fancy schmancy mansion like that — ' "

"We weren't thrown out of our house, Mrs. Carvelli."

The woman barely stopped to breathe. "There but for the grace of God, I say. We could be in the same rowboat without the oars, you know what I mean? So what is it you need, honey?"

Eleanor spoke each word as if it were followed by a period. "I — need — a — job. At — the — G.E.—That's all."

"Well, sure. Of course. Why didn't you tell me before? I could've helped out. But you don't want no job at the G.E.. That's not for some doctor's daughter, huh? Ernie — he's my brother — he's always looking for help in that office of his. Summer help. He complains all the time how those secretaries are too high and mighty to do their own filing."

"Your brother needs someone to file? In his office?"

"His *insurance* office. Porzio's Insurance," Mrs. Carvelli said proudly. "He's a big shot insurance man. Brick building right downtown, by Trembley Street and Bell Circle. You go see him this morning. I'll go right in and call him, tell him you're coming."

"I can't bring Lindy with me, Mrs. Carvelli."

"Hey. You just send her downstairs when you're leaving. I

got a whole plate of cannolis waiting to be eaten. No skin off my nose. I'm not doing anything else in the world the whole day long."

Mrs. Carvelli would be doing nothing else, except filling Lindy with all the food and attention Mama couldn't give her. Soon Lindy would belong to Mrs. Carvelli more than she did to Eleanor and Mama. What if Lindy forgot about Daddy completely? And the house in Cape Ann — and how Eleanor looked before the fire? But the picture of Mama arriving home every night, hair frizzled and eyelids drooping, filled Eleanor's mind. "I'll send her right down," she said.

Mrs. Carvelli waited on the front porch for Lindy and Eleanor. "They're passing along the message to Ernie. You're all set," she said. "You, Lindy, you scoot along inside. I got something special inside for you." She pushed Lindy toward the door. "But you gotta wash your hands first like a lady." Mrs. Carvelli waited until Lindy disappeared into the apartment. "You never know what they get into, kids these days. Picking up all kinds of stuff and putting it into their mouths."

She placed a package wrapped with brown paper and string into Eleanor's hands. "Here! For you. A sandwich and a piece of cake. In case you get hungry on the way. Sheesh, you young girls. Too skinny. In my day, men liked a little meat on their girls."

"Thank you, Mrs. Carvelli."

"Your Mama, she would've done the same. I'm just filling in for the time being. " Her voice sounded gravelly, as if she spent too much time shouting neighborhood gossip to Mrs. McIntire two houses away.

And now Eleanor's voice wouldn't work properly, either. She tried to say thank you again, but all that came out was a gurgle. She had to turn away suddenly and hurry down the porch, before Mrs. Carvelli noticed the glistening in Eleanor's eyes and asked, "You got a rock in your eye?"

Eleanor looked up at the three-story brick building at the corner of Trembley Street and Bell Circle. She expected to see a huge neon sign flashing once a second, advertising the "Big Shot Insurance Man." No sign greeted her. She crossed the street, searched the first two blocks, around the corner, and crossed back to the building again. Still no Porzio's sign. Words painted above one storefront said "Byrd's Pastry and Bake Shop." More ornate letters next to an open door read "Carberry's Jewelry."

Mrs. Carvelli must have invented Ernie. That or she hadn't seen him in so many years that the man had moved lock, stock, and barrel to another location, maybe to avoid his sister's chattering.

Finally, on a door next to the bakery window, Eleanor spotted gold lettering on a black sign: "Porzio Insurance Agency, Second Floor."

But she couldn't walk through that door. Not yet. Instead, she retraced her steps until she was standing in front of Byrd's Bakery again. At least in front of the bakery she could steady her legs while pretending to inspect the breads and rolls cooling in the display case.

And she could practice her smile, too. It came out crooked sometimes, especially when she was nervous or tired. The muscles in her cheek and chin pulled at the corner of her mouth, as if the dentist had shot her with too much Novocain. Some days, she had to smile based on memory alone.

And her mouth was tired today. She had smiled so much already. She'd smiled at the streetcar conductor who wouldn't touch her money. "Keep it," he said. He leaned away from her as if she had some contagious disease.

She had smiled at the policeman directing traffic on the corner of Whittin Avenue. He stopped traffic for her and helped her across the street, the way he would help a crippled person who couldn't do anything for herself.

One of the bakery ladies, wearing a white apron and a smudge of flour on her chin, placed another tray of rolls alongside the bread. Eleanor stepped back from the window. She could imagine the scene otherwise — the woman looking up and seeing her, the tray dropping, rolls falling all over the place, and the woman's mouth widening into an "O." And all the time, Eleanor would wear an apologetic smile on her face. "I'm sorry," her smile would say. "I didn't mean to startle you."

Eleanor turned and headed back to Porzio's. She walked through the brass-trimmed doors and into a lobby that smelled more like a bakery than an insurance office. Her shoes tapped against a black marble floor as she walked toward the wide staircase that curved up to the next floor.

She shifted Mrs. Carvelli's package into her left hand as she climbed the steps. At the landing, she hesitated. *Mrs. Carvelli must have described your face in excruciating detail,* she reminded herself as she stood facing a double set of glass doors. But her feet still weighed a thousand pounds each as she walked through those doors, and by the time she reached the receptionist's desk, she thought she would never be able to move them again.

The receptionist barely lifted her head. "Yes?"

"I'm here to see . . ." Mrs. Carvelli hadn't told Eleanor whom she should see. "It's about a job. My name is Eleanor Driscoll. Mr. Porzio is expecting me."

The receptionist shook her head. "That can't be. He's not in the office today."

"It's for filing. Things like that. Mr. Porzio's sister sent me. She said he was looking for someone." The weight in Eleanor's feet spread to her whole body — her fingers, her shoulders, even the corners of her mouth.

For the first time, the receptionist's eyes focused on Eleanor. They flickered away for a moment, then settled again on Eleanor's face. She nodded toward an armchair by her desk. "Why don't you take a seat right here, Miss Driscoll? I'll see if I can buzz Mrs. Bernard. She's in charge of hiring secretaries anyway. I'm sure she'll see you."

"I'm — I'm not really a — a secretary," Eleanor stammered. "I'm really here just for a summer job — filing and sorting."

"Mrs. Bernard is the office manager. She interviews all our help," the receptionist said. In a gentler voice she added, "I wouldn't worry, though. We haven't had any luck finding anyone. Not too many young girls are interested in filing and sorting — not when they can make more money in a factory somewhere."

Eleanor placed Mrs. Carvelli's bundle on the floor next to her and sat in the chair by the receptionist's desk. She watched as the woman lifted the phone from its cradle and spoke into it. "I have a Miss Driscoll here to see you about that summer job. She says Mr. Porzio's sister called about this."

Eleanor tapped her fingers, first on her skirt and then on the arms of the chair. On the wall opposite her seat, a clock ticked away the time in slow motion. Ten minutes, then fifteen minutes passed. People hurried from office to office. A tall man, too skinny everywhere except his stomach, stopped at the receptionist's desk. He glanced quickly at Eleanor and then bent low to whisper into the receptionist's ear. She shook her head. "I'm not listening," she said. The man grinned and whispered again. "I'm not listening," the receptionist repeated. "That's enough." He gave up and walked back through the glass doors.

Finally, a door from one of the inner offices opened, and a brisk, attractive woman emerged. Her high heels clicked efficiently across the polished floor. She reached the receptionist's desk and laid a sheaf of papers on it. "You said we have an applicant for the job?" she asked in a clipped tone.

The receptionist nodded toward Eleanor, who stood and extended her hand. Mrs. Bernard inspected Eleanor the same way Mama chose a roast from Bailey's Market. Her eyes tightened. Her jaw set.

"I'm Pauline Bernard. Office manager." She grasped Eleanor's outstretched hand, shook it once, and abruptly let go. Then she wiped her own hand against her skirt.

A roaring like the sound of waves battering against rocks filled Eleanor's ears. She spoke a little too loudly. "My name is Eleanor Driscoll."

Pauline Bernard didn't bother to take Eleanor through the

open doors and into an inner office. Instead, she stood leaning slightly to one side and said, "Of course you've had experience at this sort of thing."

"You're looking for someone to file. I can handle that."

The woman's mouth smiled. Her eyes did not. "We sometimes have extra typing. Our secretaries work very hard, and we like to give them a little help if we can." Eleanor glanced at the receptionist, whose eyes widened and darted from Mrs. Bernard's face to the blotter on her desk.

"That was not my understanding of the job," Eleanor said.

"Well . . ." Mrs. Bernard's lips formed that same false smile. "People don't always explain things very well, do they?" Her voice sliced through Eleanor. "We are interviewing quite a few other girls this afternoon. We'll be getting back to you as soon as possible. Very nice meeting you, Miss Driscoll.

The roaring in Eleanor's ears returned. "I'm sure it was, Mrs. Bernard," she said.

The office manager turned on her spindly heels and disappeared through the inner doors.

Eleanor turned toward the receptionist. Trying desperately to control her voice, she asked, "Should I leave my number? For someone to call me?" As if it mattered now.

"Miss Driscoll? I'm sorry. I mean, yes, please. I am sorry. I didn't understand what the job involved." The poor woman looked truly embarrassed and helpless. She pushed a slip of paper in front of Eleanor and handed her a pencil. "I'm really sorry," she repeated.

Eleanor spit out her answer. "I understand completely." Her

eyes could barely focus on the paper, and she wrote her name and "TU4-2673" in a huge, childish scrawl. Mrs. Carvelli's care package lay on the floor next to her chair. Let it stay there, for all she cared.

She didn't need anything to remind her of this awful day.

Chapter Three

❧ ❧

On the Tremont Avenue streetcar, Eleanor leaned her shoulder and head against the window. Passengers waiting at each stop had a perfect view of her face, but Eleanor didn't care. The car stopped and started and stopped and started again. Its lurching made her cheek bump against the glass. She didn't care about that, either. All she cared about was Pauline Bernard and her hard eyes, Pauline Bernard and her snippy voice.

I hope ants get hungry some night and crawl over your face and eat off your make-up while you're sleeping.

I hope you cross the street in front of a taxi at a red light during rush hour.

I hope you are standing in front of the Essex Street theater some busy Saturday night and your skirt falls right down around your ankles.

The Pauline Bernard Most Appropriate Punishment litany

went on longer than the Litany of Saints from the Easter Vigil service. And it would never pass Father Berube's "Prayers should be for the praise and glory of God" test.

What a truly mean, hateful woman. Pauline Bernard wasn't a people storm. She was the hurricane of '38, smashing Eleanor's feelings to smithereens the way the hurricane had smashed houses and trees. But Mrs. Bernard wasn't the only person grinding away at Eleanor. If only Mrs. Carvelli had minded her own business, Eleanor never would have gone down to Porzio's Insurance and met that awful woman.

When the streetcar pulled up to the curb at Everett Street, Eleanor could barely step off the car and onto the pavement. Her knees wouldn't straighten properly — not when the streetcar left, not when another one came by and another one after that. But she couldn't stand here all day long. If she didn't get home soon, Lindy would be saying, "Sheesh" and telling everyone her name was Lindy Carvelli. Besides, what if the man in the corner house came out to check on her? His eyes would look everywhere except at her face when he asked, "Are you all right, miss?"

Eleanor didn't have any pretend smiles left — or any thank-yous or any of the other polite words people expected her to say even when their words shredded her feelings.

Nothing to worry about, Mr. Never-Look-at-My Face. It's just the freak show on the corner of Everett and Pine. Buy your tickets. Ten cents a peek at the living wax girl.

If she could just be alone for a while. If she could sit in the darkness of her bedroom and hide from everyone. If only the sun would disappear behind clouds so dark that they chased everyone from the beach, she could escape to Mahoney's Point and take off her shoes and let the water trickle through her toes.

Droplets of sweat trickled down Eleanor's neck onto her back. "Young ladies perspire. They don't sweat," Grams had intoned, as if she were reciting one of the commandments. But Grams lived in that Cape Ann world, not this Beachmont one. Here, people sweat. On the streetcar, they stood so close to Eleanor that her nose wrinkled at the smell.

That was the whole problem with Beachmont. People got too close. They crowded onto every inch of space. And they built their neighborhoods the same way, two- and three-family houses that had no room between them, no room for breathing. Eleanor couldn't blink an eye without someone noticing.

When she got to the apartment, Lindy and Mrs. Carvelli would be sitting on the front porch waiting for her. Mrs. Carvelli's first words would be, "So, my brother paying you enough?" Lindy's face would glow with pride. *There's my big shot sister with her new job.* Eleanor didn't need Lindy's pride. She needed to breathe. She needed space. She needed . . . Eleanor pulled her arms close to her body and folded them across her chest. She didn't know what she needed.

Daddy! Of course! Her whole body ached with longing. She could wear a million scars on her face, but Daddy would always see the real Eleanor. The way he did that night at the Palm Gardens. *Oh, Eleanor. The night you were born, when I held you in my arms for the first time, sweetheart, I was so afraid. I was afraid of dropping you, afraid of making mistakes, afraid of not being the kind of father I should be. Then your eyes looked straight into mine with such love. They told us in medical school that babies can't focus their eyes for the first three months — that they don't feel emotions. But I knew differently. You had such a giving heart from the very beginning."* He bent down and kissed her forehead. *"You still do, Eleanor. You make me so proud.*

Eleanor started down Everett Street. "Daddy, you're the one who made *me* proud." She repeated the words over and over again, until they had a certain rhythm. She let the rhythm carry her toward the house, toward Lindy and Mrs. Carvelli. But she walked almost as slowly as Mr. Partenope. She checked the sky every few steps, searching for a cloud, a shadow, anything that would deluge the Point and send everyone scurrying for cover. Because she knew if she could just be alone, sitting on the sea wall and letting the smell of the beach roses fill her, she would find Daddy again in the gentle lap of wave against sand.

No Lindy and Mrs. Carvelli sat on the front porch or the back stoop; no Lindy and Mrs. Carvelli called out to her from the Carvellis' apartment. Eleanor couldn't hear Lindy's giggling or Mrs. Carvelli's belly laugh as she headed up the back stairs. Perhaps they had gone to the drugstore. Mrs. Carvelli liked to feed Lindy free ice-cream sodas from the drugstore that her husband owned. *Good.* Eleanor would have time to think up some lie before Lindy came bounding in asking about the job.

A pile of envelopes lay on the kitchen table. Eleanor shuffled through the pile. Mail was like the newsreels at the beginning of movies. It announced every detail of a person's life. Mama used to receive S.S. Pierce catalogs and cream-colored envelopes with embossed initials. Daddy received the *Atlantic Monthly* and brochures for tongue depressors from Purington's Medical Supplies. The post office still forwarded brochures about the best tongue depressors to Daddy, but Mama hadn't received a catalog from S.S. Pierce in months. And all of her envelopes were yellow, for bills yet to be paid.

Eleanor stopped shuffling. Her heart thumped against her chest. There, at the bottom of the pile, she spotted a blue and red border. *Robert!*

She traced his name and his address with the tips of her fingers. *How did you know?* she wanted to ask him. *How did you know I would need you today?* She wondered, just for a moment, whether Mrs. Carvelli had seen the letter. Because if she had, the whole world would know about Robert. "Did you tell him about your face, Eleanor?" That's what everyone would ask.

But that was a worry for some other time. Not now. Now she had Robert's words, filling her with a safety she hadn't felt since Daddy died.

June 12, 1944

Dear Eleanor,

What a beautiful early summer day here! People think of New York as this great big city, all buildings and steel. But from the City College campus, New York looks as green as Grafton Park back home, with its trees and flowers. I even hear birds. I never paid much attention to them before.

You would make a terrific nurse, Eleanor. You're smart, and you understand people's feelings. Believe it or not, I played around with the idea of becoming a doctor for a while, but it would mean too many years of studying. I just wanted to get a degree and then say good-bye to school. I should say, my parents wanted me to get a degree. I come from a long line of teachers. Too long. That's the one thing I've decided never to be.

Perhaps when I get out of here, I'll go back for some pre-med courses after all.

Don't worry, Eleanor. You can complain all you want to me. I don't mind. I would want to strangle Mrs. Carvelli, too. Perhaps we could have adjoining cells. I'm just teasing. Don't let her get to you, though. She sounds like one of those people who believes it is her mission in life to tell everybody else how to live. Your mother is probably right that Mrs. Carvelli means well, but that doesn't make her easy to take.

I'm sorry. I don't mean to play the big brother.

Take care of yourself, Eleanor.

> *Affectionately,*
> *Robert*

Eleanor touched the word. *Affectionately.* Insane, maybe, but she could feel its warmth, as if Robert had somehow reached across hundreds of miles and said the word instead of writing it.

In the safety of her bedroom, she read the letter over and over until Robert's words were as familiar as the songs she heard on the radio. Someone who wanted to be a doctor, who made her heart beat the way it did, could never hurt her the way Pauline Bernard had. Not that Eleanor would give him the chance. She had learned her lesson. Daddy always said she was a quick learner.

But she could pretend. Eleanor lay across her bed and imagined Robert as an intern at Boston General, making the morning rounds. He was tall, with wide shoulders and long fingers that he ran through his dark hair whenever he was puzzled about something. She was the charge nurse, quiet and efficient.

"You've done a wonderful job with this patient, nurse. You saved his life, " Robert said as he stood in front of a man with a tracheotomy. His voice held a certain admiration. "Miss Driscoll. Hmm. I used to write to someone with that last name."

She wouldn't tell him then. She would wait until some lunchtime when he was searching for a place to sit. "You don't mind if I join you?" He had a deep, gentle voice and his patients, especially the children, adored him.

Eleanor shook her head, her mouth full of lettuce and tomato and bread, and he placed his tray beside hers, not across from hers.

He lifted the dishes from his tray and put them on the table. Then he sat next to her, his body almost touching hers. His hands, with those beautiful long fingers, lay on either side of his plate. "Hey! We chose the same lunch! Exactly," he said. "How's that for coincidence? It's like we read each other's minds or something."

Or something.

That's when she would tell him. "I'm Eleanor Driscoll. *The*

Eleanor Driscoll. *Your* Eleanor Driscoll." Eleanor had practiced the words so many times that they were engraved on her mind. But no matter how many hundreds of times she practiced, she could never quite say them out loud. Because she could never quite imagine the ending. It was like one of those dreams where she imagined herself falling from the highest branch of a tree. Always, right before she landed, *splat,* on the ground below, she awoke. Someone — maybe Jack Carmody, maybe Marybeth — had told her once, "If you actually land, that means you are dead."

"Hey! Eleanor! You back yet? Eleanor?" Mrs. Carvelli called from the kitchen.

In a minute, Mrs. Carvelli would wander down the hall and into the bedroom. The thought of Mrs. Carvelli nosing her way around Eleanor's things was too much to handle.

"I'll be right there," Eleanor called back. She walked out to the living room where Mrs. Carvelli waited, hands on her hips.

"Hey, Eleanor. You look just like those working girls. Like that Rosemary Russell woman in the movies. Don't Eleanor look good, considering?" She poked Lindy.

"Eleanor always looks good," Lindy said.

Lindy couldn't possibly believe that, could she? Eleanor could always tell when Lindy was lying, because she tucked her right cheek against her shoulder in order to avoid people's eyes. But Lindy was gazing right up at Eleanor with a pride that stung far more than Pauline Bernard's rudeness.

Mrs. Carvelli was still talking. "So, how much money is Ernie paying you, Eleanor? You should've asked for more."

"I didn't get the job, Mrs. Carvelli."

"What?"

"I said I didn't get the job." All of a sudden Eleanor wanted to collapse right there on the rug. She had to steel herself to remain standing.

"They're not giving you the job? That's nuts! I left a message for Ernie. They were supposed to pass it along."

"Your brother wasn't there, Mrs. Carvelli. I had to see the office manager, Pauline Bernard. She wasn't interested in hiring someone like me."

Mrs. Carvelli considered for a moment and then declared, "Hey, Eleanor, you don't want that job anyway. A stupid job with stupid people like that whatever-her-name is. I spit on people that stupid." She spit into her hand. "You don't need nobody like that."

"You're absolutely right, Mrs. Carvelli. I don't need *anybody*."

Mrs. Carvelli might have had more to say, but Eleanor didn't hear her. She couldn't remember returning to the bedroom or even falling asleep on her bed. And when she finally woke, she had the hardest time realizing that she was no longer dancing with Daddy in a magical room that sparkled like a thousand diamonds.

Revolving doors. Chandeliers sparkling like a hundred prisms. Crystal goblets filled with water that waiters carry on trays high above their heads — so high it seems as if the trays float across the room. The waiters in their snow-white coats weave their way through tables set with snow-white

46

tablecloths. When Eleanor squints, the shine from the silver place settings and the jewelry on women's necks and arms and fingers becomes pieces of stars that have dropped from heaven. Special presents just for her.

She smooths her velvet skirt with its petticoat so full that it flares out even though she is seated. And she bounces a little in her chair, like a small girl at her first party, too excited to sit still. Except she's not a small girl anymore. She's sixteen. And tonight is Daddy's gift to her.

She touches her dress again. Wine-colored velvet. It's Mama's dress, really. Girls with red hair shouldn't wear shades of red, but Mama says Eleanor's hair is more auburn. The pearl necklace that warms Eleanor's collarbone belongs to Mama, too, but the earrings are Eleanor's own, dangling prisms of diamond chips and gold. She rolls her head gently back and forth to feel their luxuriousness against her neck.

Other women touch their hair, too, rolling their heads back and forth — so many women in elegant dresses, allowing their escorts to whirl them onto the dance floor. Soldiers in crisp uniforms jam themselves along the back wall and wait patiently for their chance. "It doesn't seem right, Daddy," Eleanor says. "Are we selfish to be so happy when so many bad things are going on in the world?"

Daddy touches her cheek. "Sweetheart, happiness is always right. Otherwise Hitler wins. And we can't let that happen. Eleanor, I want you to laugh and dance your whole life long. I want you always to be as happy as you are right at this moment."

The music never stops, and they dance and eat and drink

and then dance again. The waiter brings fancy shrimp cocktails on melting ice and bows low when he collects the plates. Eleanor's ginger ale grows warm as it sits on the table, but Daddy says his old-fashioned is just fine, thank you very much, and does Eleanor want to dance again? Does she want to dance again? Oh, she could glide across the floor forever without ever feeling her feet! She is Cinderella at the ball. Any moment a tall, handsome prince will reach out his hand and ask her to waltz with him. And Eleanor will tell him, "Perhaps later. This dance is for my father."

Because tonight is Daddy's night, too. That's what he says as they dance. "We won't have many more chances to be together like this, sweetheart," Daddy says. "So you don't mind dancing with your old man? Just this one last time?"

"I will never mind dancing with you, Daddy," Eleanor whispers. But he can't hear. Too many people are trying to talk over the music. And the music never stops. The orchestra plays "Moonlight and roses . . . bring wonderful memories of you."

The music kept revolving around her mind, calling her back to sleep, back to the enchantment. *Daddy? Where are you, Daddy?* Eleanor's eyes opened wide. *Lindy? Mama?*

She burst into the kitchen, where the two sat quietly, Lindy snuggled in the curve of her mother's arm. "You are my sunshine," Mama sang softly as her hand stroked Lindy's hair. She stopped singing when Eleanor entered the room. In a careful tone she said, "Hi, sweetie."

The muscle in Eleanor's right eye twitched. *Mama knows. Mrs. Bigmouth Carvelli just couldn't wait to tell her about me not getting the job. And she'll tell the whole world. I'm too ugly to be with other people, too ugly to work. Even Mama thinks so.*

Lindy burrowed her head deeper into Mama's chest. "Mommy's been singing to me. She has a pretty voice, doesn't she, Ellie." In a sleepy voice, she sang the words, "You make me happy when skies are gray." Eleanor had to clench her fists to keep from covering her ears.

Mama said, "I didn't bother waking you for supper. I thought you needed the sleep more." She didn't look at Eleanor. "Mr. Carvelli was here a while ago. He wanted to ask you something about a job. I told him whatever he had to say could wait until later."

Mr. Carvelli waited an hour before he knocked on the kitchen door again. The minute Eleanor opened it, he whipped off his hat and held it in front of him. His hands kept fidgeting with that hat. They rolled the brim and creased the top. "I need to talk with you, Eleanor," he said. "I need to ask you for this favor. I need to ask if you will please do me the honor of working at my pharmacy."

His eyes never once looked up from the floor, but he wasn't being rude. His eyes never met Mama's face, either. Eleanor began to answer, "Mr. Carvelli — " She had to stop. The right words wouldn't come. She tried again. "Mr. Carvelli, I would be honored to work for you."

Mr. Carvelli's smile warmed the entire room. She thought about that smile later as she sat at the kitchen table, fountain pen in hand, Mama's best stationery spread in front of her.

June 14, 1944

Dear Robert,

Guess what! Tonight, Mr. Carvelli asked me to work part-time in his pharmacy. He says that Mrs. Carvelli is tired of doing all the paperwork. She wants to go back to school to get her high school diploma.

Carvelli's is my first job, so I'm a bit nervous. But I won't mind working with Mr. Carvelli. He is as quiet as his wife is loud. He actually reminds me of an undertaker, the way he always wears a black suit coat and black hat.

Mr. Carvelli was very kind to give me a job. However, I'm sure the idea came from his wife. I complain about her a lot. But she does have a "heart of gold," as my father would have said.

Mrs. Carvelli wants to learn how to drive a car! Can you believe that? Mrs. Carvelli behind the steering wheel of a car? I can't help thinking she would make the perfect secret weapon — for the Germans. There's no legal way to prevent such a disaster from happening. Pharmacists aren't affected by gas rationing.

I will admit that part of my complaining is because I am extremely jealous. I always wanted to drive a car. I like the idea of having the freedom to go wherever I want whenever I want.

It's getting late, so I had better say good-bye. But I just had to tell you: if you don't hear from me for a while, it may be because I'm hiding from Secret Weapon Angela.

Please stay safe! I'll try to do the same.

Affectionately,
Eleanor

Chapter Four

❧ ❧

Rain splashed against the drugstore windows, giving everything mirrored in them the kind of halo that streetlights wore on foggy evenings. Mr. Carvelli's reflection wore one of those halos. Eleanor sat on a stool behind the back counter and watched in the windows as he carefully removed his hat and his suitcoat. The way his black hair was plastered against his skull made him look younger somehow, like a little boy who had been caught in a downpour. With surprising vanity, he leaned down to check his reflection in the counter's chrome edging. Eleanor's heart twisted. Daddy used to do that. Between patients, he used the chrome edging on the examining table in his office to check his hair and teeth, and to straighten his tie.

She had to look away, let her eyes rest anywhere else. They settled for a moment on her own image. The windows were too hazy to show her scars, but she could see her blue-and-white jumper, and her hands folded over crossed knees. Mama would not be happy with that. "A lady crosses only her ankles," she had reminded Eleanor just yesterday.

Eleanor examined the rest of the store through the window's reflection. The mist distorted everything. The cardboard Aqua Velva man resembled someone standing in front of one of those crazy mirrors at Beachmont Park. The steel edges on the soda fountain's counter appeared blanket soft, and the aspirin display was lost in a blur of light and color that rippled as raindrops dripped down the glass and out of sight.

The windows couldn't reflect the smell, however. Eleanor's nose wrinkled at the irritating aroma of stale cigarette smoke mixed with just a hint of eucalyptus. The smell reminded her that people she had never met, people who might be horrified by her face, would soon come into the drugstore.

Her toes were pinched against the leather of her shoes, and she wiggled them back and forth as if she were trying to free a loose baby tooth. Mama had bought new saddle shoes for Eleanor to wear home from the hospital. She hadn't worn them again until today.

She hadn't even wanted to wear them today. She hadn't wanted to get up or get dressed or put on these new shoes. Any excitement she felt about the job had melted into a puddle of what-ifs. What if the other employees were like Pauline Bernard? What if they couldn't stand being near her? What if Mr. Carvelli hadn't warned anyone what she looked like? They would come waltzing into the store and stop dead in their tracks the minute they saw her.

But Mama had been so eager. She had already told the

hospital she would be working fewer hours. "I just know you'll have a good day, sweetie," Mama had said as she waved good-bye.

It was the "I just know" that had pushed the fear out of Eleanor's mind. *Money.* That's what it came down to. If she worked hard enough, Mr. Carvelli might give her more hours. Then she and Mama and Lindy would be drowning in dollar bills — dollars to buy food that Mama didn't have to cook, dollars to buy new shoes for Lindy, a sweater for herself, maybe bath soap for Mama.

Eleanor uncrossed her legs and smoothed her skirt over her knees. All right. So maybe people would stop dead in their tracks. What was Mr. Carvelli supposed to do? Place a sign in the window warning customers? *Burn Victim on Premises. Hide Your Eyes.* They would get used to seeing her. Angela Carvelli had. And Mr. Partenope, too — sort of.

A large woman with gray hair pushed her way in through the front door. She trudged up the center aisle as if she knew exactly what to expect in life. She stopped for a moment to shake off her umbrella and raincoat. She mumbled something to herself about "nuisance," and "God-awful rain," then called out to Mr. Carvelli, "Raining enough to drown a goat! It'll be a quiet morning, this one. I can tell you that right now."

Then she continued her trek, straightening birthday cards, poking at jars of petroleum jelly and stomach medicine as she went. "We'll have to get Clarice or Susan or whoever works this afternoon to dust in here. Nothing worse than reaching for a bottle of Pepto Bismol that looks like it's been sitting on the shelf for a year." She cackled loudly. "Even if it has."

Mr. Carvelli stepped out from behind his counter. "Mrs. Williams. It's you," he said, glancing uncertainly at Eleanor.

Mrs. Williams turned in Eleanor's direction. She gave a tiny squeak as she caught her breath.

"This is our upstairs neighbor," Mr. Carvelli said. "This is Eleanor. She's going to be working here. She'll attack that pile of prescriptions we've been building up." He patted Eleanor's shoulder awkwardly. "She knows something about drugstores already. Her father was a doctor."

Mrs. Williams nodded. "That's nice. We've been needing an extra pair of hands around here." Her eyes were riveted to Eleanor's face. Well, Eleanor could be rude, too. Her jaw muscles tightened, and she stared right back at Mrs. Williams. There would be no fake smiles this morning.

Then, as if someone had popped a balloon somewhere behind her and brought her back into the real world, Mrs. Williams' manner changed. "You've been sitting here all this time, and I bet Chubbs never showed you the lavatory where you can freshen up. Look at you, your hair all damp like a wet puppy. Come with me. I'll give you a tour of the place."

Eleanor followed Mrs. Williams through to the back room and into the storage area, where a tiny bathroom was located. The woman talked nonstop the whole time.

"I pretty much run things. Until late afternoon, that is. That's when the youngsters take over. Of course Rosemary Myers comes in to help with the noontime crowd, but I swear that woman is more of a hindrance than a help. She spends altogether too much time talking with the customers and then complaining about how much work she's doing. Lord, I could feed an army in the time it takes her to pour a cup of coffee. But help's help these days, I suppose. Until she gets here, though, I'm pretty much it. I've been with Chubbs — what is it now — seventeen years come September. I do everything except give out drugs."

"Mr. Carvelli said I would mostly copy prescriptions in the back. I'm not taking your job, am I?" Eleanor asked.

For a moment, Mrs. Williams looked like Grams did every time she patted Eleanor's scarred cheek. "Oh, honey, don't be silly. It's about time he hired someone in here to help with the paperwork. We're so behind." She pointed to stacks of prescriptions hiding most of a battered wooden desk.

"These all have to be copied onto our customers' record cards. That job alone will keep you busy for weeks. We're over six months behind. Carvelli's is a pretty busy place, and I have to admit, we all hate doing the cards. It's just so hard reading the doctors' handwriting. You'd think they'd teach them something useful in medical school, like penmanship." Mrs. Williams coughed. "I'm sorry, Eleanor. I forgot. Chubbs said your father was a doctor."

"I don't mind, Mrs. Williams. If I could read Daddy's handwriting, I can read anyone's."

"Your father was a nice man, I'm sure."

"Yes. He was." It felt strange talking about Daddy so matter-of-factly, not in the hallowed tones that everyone else used.

Mr. Carvelli poked his head inside the door. "Ah, Eleanor. Mrs. Williams has been showing you around?"

"I've been showing her the prescription stack, Chubbs."

They both shuddered. "Mrs. Williams, we don't want to frighten her away so soon. We don't want her to quit the first hour of her first day at work."

Eleanor spent the whole morning copying prescriptions onto cards. Mrs. Williams had to show Eleanor what to do only once. But some of the doctors' writing was unreadable, and a few times she had to ask Mr. Carvelli to interpret for her. "I don't like to keep bothering you," she said after the third interruption.

Mr. Carvelli shook his head. "No, no. I don't mind at all."

There was such safety in the monotony of writing. Pick up a prescription, decipher the writing, copy the information onto a card. Repeat the process. Again. Again. Eleanor's neck ached. Her fingers cramped.

She stretched her fingers across the desk in front of her. The store had suddenly become busy with customers. They called out their greetings to Mrs. Williams as they scraped their feet on the mat by the front door. "How you doing, Mrs. W.?" Eleanor's muscles tensed, waiting for someone to barge into her cubby demanding, "Who are you? What are you doing here?"

But nobody came near her, and Eleanor relaxed. *Safe.* Like writing to Robert was safe. On the desk blotter, in the top righthand corner, she printed *RB* in tiny letters. Then she printed his initials again, a little larger, in every other corner of the page: *RB,* punctuated by a daisy where the periods should have been.

She was still drawing when Mrs. Williams turned on the soda fountain's grill. *Fire!* The smell spun through Eleanor's head, making her so sick with fear that she had to close her eyes and grab onto the desk with both hands. *Mrs. Williams is cooking, Eleanor. It's not a fire. You'll be fine. If you just count to twenty, to thirty. Take deep breaths.* She forced herself to inhale and exhale the way she had when she was six and just learning to swim. Slowly, the nausea passed.

Her hand reached for the next prescription. *Daddy!* Eleanor couldn't mistake that writing — the same black letters, the same tight signature with its looping *T*. Sometimes, for coke syrup or cough medicine, he wrote prescriptions for patients and extended them for months. "You don't need to see a doctor every time your supper doesn't agree with you," he always told them. But she never knew he had patients who lived so near Beachmont. Quickly she raised the paper to her nose and sniffed. Nothing of Daddy remained — no precious aroma of Ferguson's tobacco or peppermint Lifesavers.

Daddy!

It was the first word Eleanor had spoken when she awoke after the fire.

Mama had sat in a steel-framed chair beside the bed. One of her hands curled around Eleanor's wrist, stroking the skin with her thumb.

"Shh. Don't talk, Eleanor. You need your rest."

Eleanor's eyes focused on the chair, the glass pitcher on a table by the window, white figures rustling by the open door. "Daddy?" Her voice felt fuzzy and distant, like a bad telephone connection.

"He's not here, sweetie."

Everything looked shiny and clean. Eleanor smelled rubbing alcohol. That's what nurses used to make things sparkle. "I'm in the hospital? I've been hurt?" she asked.

"Yes, Eleanor."

"And Daddy? Is he in the hospital, too?"

Mama smoothed Eleanor's forehead with hands as cold as icicles. "I told you, sweetie. Daddy's not here."

But Eleanor had to check for herself. No Daddy standing by the door, no Daddy sitting by the window, no Daddy warming the stark walls and the polished floor with his presence.

Because of the flames — of course. They had roared like the loudest train engine, lit up the Palm Gardens brighter than a thousand suns. Daddy had said, "Don't watch the fire, Eleanor. Watch me. Hold onto my hands."

And she had. For as long as she could.

"Is Daddy in another hospital?" Eleanor asked. "I remember a little bit. I looked for him, Mama. All the time I was in the hallway with all those beds. I kept looking and looking, but Daddy wasn't there."

"Sweetie, I don't know how to tell you this." Mama tried to touch Eleanor's shoulder, but Eleanor pulled away.

"No," she whispered. Eleanor hadn't held onto Daddy's hands the way he told her to. She hadn't watched carefully enough. She had tried so hard. But people kept pushing her, shoving her. Then there were no hands left to hold; there was no Daddy left to watch.

"Daddy was very badly hurt in the fire, Eleanor."

Eleanor covered her hands with her ears. "No!" she whispered again. She couldn't let Mama say the words. If Mama said them, they would be true. And they couldn't be true. Daddy *couldn't* be dead. Eleanor would have known. She would have felt a huge, gaping wound, ripping her apart.

"No, no, no!" she had shouted, until her voice grew too hoarse to make a sound. And even after that, after Mama rocked Eleanor against her chest, after Dr. Gilligan gave her a shot — "To help you sleep," he said—Eleanor's mouth still formed the word. "No!"

A blond woman wearing a white uniform and a pink apron hurried into the back room. Eleanor turned her face to hide her wet cheeks. "I'm late," the woman announced. "Mrs. Williams will have my skin." She threw off her sweater and disappeared around the counter. Eleanor would have sworn the blond woman hadn't caught a glimpse of her face until she heard the woman ask Mrs. Williams, "Who's that? Another one of Chubbs' charity cases?"

Mrs. Williams' answer was muffled but angry. The blonde woman apologized quickly. "I only meant it as a joke." Then she must have turned to a customer. "How are you today, Ed? You feel like a couple of grilled cheese sandwiches? Maybe some Wise potato chips for such a wise guy?"

The customer chuckled. "You're a real card, Rosemary."

Eleanor forced herself to stop listening. Her trembling fingers still grasped Daddy's prescription. *It's just so hard without you, Daddy.* She couldn't place the prescription in the pile with the others. Instead, she lay the slip of paper beside her on the desk. For the longest time, she kept track of prescriptions by saying, "This is the twentieth card I've written since Daddy's. This is the twenty-first."

The buzz of the lunch crowd's chatter disappeared; the

clatter of dishes faded. Rosemary pushed her way through the doorway and grabbed her sweater off the rack. "Three o'clock and all is well, at least for this hard-working gal." She paused. "I'm Rosemary Myers, by the way." She examined the bright red polish on her fingernails. "You know, I was thinking about you. They have this make-up that covers stuff up, you know what I mean? Like pimples?" She giggled. "Well, we're not talking pimples here, are we? Anyway. You buy some of that and then get on with your life, know what I'm saying? You buy some make-up. You wear your hair down, so's it'll cover your face better, Veronica Lake style — and she don't even have your problem."

Blood. The woman's fingers could have been some beast's claws after it had finished devouring its prey. Eleanor's pencil traced the scrollwork on the desk blotter, the intricate little curves and curls, the ornate *P* for Purington's Medical Supplies. She bent her head low over the desk. But Rosemary wasn't finished.

"You got yourself a nice little job here, where people won't be staring at you all the time."

"Rosemary!" Mrs. Williams stood in the doorway. She glared at Rosemary with eyes that could have burned through ice.

"Ahh, she knows what I mean. Don't you, Eleanor? That's your name, isn't it?"

Mrs. Williams opened her mouth, but Eleanor interrupted. "It's all right." To Rosemary, she said, "I understand exactly what you mean. Rosemary, isn't it? I'll just hide away in my little cubby here and not bother anyone."

"See?" Rosemary's voice was triumphant. "Eleanor here,

she understands." Then she disappeared into the store.

Mrs. Williams stood for the longest time. "You just can't insult the Rosemarys of this world," she said. "Honey, you must be starving. You get out here and get yourself a sandwich."

"I'm really not very hungry, but thank you."

Mrs. Williams shook her head. "My son, Michael, I swear. He can eat a hundred times a day and still be hungry. Hard to get used to him not being around."

"Is he in the service?"

Eleanor swore that Mrs. Williams grew at least an inch, the way she pushed her chin up so high. "My Michael is a Marine," she said. She patted Eleanor's shoulder. "I'd best be checking on things out front before I leave. You just holler if you need anything."

Mama was sitting at the table with the *Boston Globe* spread in front of her when Eleanor walked through the back door. "How did your day go?" Mama asked. Her hands reached out to cover the story she had been reading, but Eleanor could still make out the headline: "Prison Term Expected for Palm Gardens Owner."

Eleanor's whole body slumped. "Work went fine," she said. Mama devoured every detail of the fire the way she used to devour the obituary pages. "The Irish sports pages," Daddy had called them. He never read death notices; Eleanor never read anything about the fire. She didn't want names attached to what had happened to her face.

"They give you enough work to keep you busy?"

"Actually, they're so far behind that I'll never catch up with all the copying. Mr. Carvelli asked me to work full time, Tuesday through Friday. So, yes, Mama. They're keeping me pretty busy."

Mama nodded. "We've got some fresh bread. We can have hamburger for supper. I know you don't like it very much, but now that they stopped rationing beef, hamburger is almost as cheap as Spam.

Eleanor started to say, "I don't hate hamburgers, Mama. I just don't like to smell them," but she was too weary to explain, and her exhaustion had spread to her stomach. "It's all right, Mama. I'm not that hungry. Mrs. Williams fed me a sandwich late this afternoon."

Lindy bounded through the back door like a puppy freed from its chain.

"So did you see sick people? Did you play with the cash register? I bet you had an ice-cream soda. Mama said they might have let you have a soda for free at the soda fountain! I'd pick strawberry with strawberry ice-cream and a strawberry on top."

Mama pulled Lindy into a chair. "Leave your sister alone, Lindy. She's had a long day. She'll tell us everything at supper."

But Eleanor could barely open her mouth during supper. She spoke in short sentences. "I met Mrs. Williams. She seems nice. Some girls my age work there, too. They all call Mr. Carvelli 'Chubbs.' The soda fountain's busy at lunch."

Eleanor couldn't tell her mother about Daddy's prescription. She couldn't tell her about Rosemary's cruel comments, either, or the way the smell of the grill made her feel. Always before, she had told everything to Mama. Or to Marybeth, her best friend before the fire.

Marybeth had tried to understand. "Can I do anything for you, Eleanor?" she asked the first day Eleanor returned to school. By lunchtime, however, she was back to her usual self. "Did you hear Billy McKenzie signed up for the navy? He stopped by one night before he left. I was so embarrassed, I thought I'd die. Me with damp hair and no lipstick. You should have seen me. Do you think he might be interested in me, anyway?"

Marybeth had short, dark curls that she straightened religiously with curlers the size of Campbell's soup cans. Eleanor didn't know what she wanted from Marybeth, but she didn't want to hear her complaining because every strand of hair on her beautiful head wasn't perfect.

"We'll always be best friends," Eleanor had told Marybeth the day the moving men came. "No matter what happens, we'll always keep in touch." But Eleanor hadn't kept in touch. She hadn't written one letter to her best friend, although Marybeth had written several to her. She hadn't returned any of Marybeth's phone calls, either. Maybe after I'm adjusted more, she told herself, knowing that she was lying. She could never adjust to this new Eleanor.

Funny though, when she sprawled across her bed with her pad of paper and Daddy's fountain pen, she had no trouble telling Robert about her new job. Oh, not about the grill and how the smell of cooking meat reminded her of the fire, but other things — the ones she was too tired to discuss with

Lindy and her mother. When had that happened? When had Robert become the person with whom she most wanted to share things?

June 15, 1944

Dear Robert,

I started work at the drugstore today.

Carvelli's is not very big, but it's about the cleanest place on earth. There might be a speck of dust elsewhere in the store, but our soda fountain is as spotless as Daddy's examining room used to be. Mrs. Williams keeps it that way. She has worked with Mr. Carvelli since before Lindbergh flew across the Atlantic!! Notice I wrote "worked with." Neither of them considers her an employee. She rules the place and insists on having everything done her way. But she's really nice, at least to me. Clarice and Susan say that's because I'm new. "Just wait," they tell me.

Actually, only one of them said it but I'm not sure which. Clarice and Susan are two girls my age who come in at three o'clock. They do everything together, even make deliveries around town. Chubbs — that's Mr. Carvelli — doesn't like to send "his girls" out alone. "You never know," he says. Clarice is tall and thin with mousy brown hair and glasses; Susan is short and round with mousy brown hair and no glasses. Or is it the other way around? I got so confused, meeting everyone and trying to finish up a pile of prescriptions before three o'clock came around that I didn't even stop for lunch.

That had been the hardest part, meeting everyone — especially Clarice and Susan. She heard them before she even saw them, two giggling, chattering girls who sounded so much like Marybeth and Eleanor used to sound that she peeked around the corner to see who was reliving her life. Mrs. Williams greeted the two midway up the aisle. She whispered something, and both girls' faces turned immediately toward Eleanor's cubby.

Eleanor pulled her head back, but not before she had locked eyes with the taller girl. The girl's eyes widened at first, but they softened into kindness.

That's how Robert's eyes would be. Startled at first, but then kind.

One of my father's prescriptions was in the pile. I didn't tell my mother, even though we talk about Daddy all the time. We talk about the summers we spent in Nahant, about how he taught Lindy to skip stones across the water's surface when she was only four years old.

Daddy was so patient. And it was such a hot afternoon. He handed Lindy stone after stone. She flung them about two feet, and they plopped underneath the water immediately. But he kept at it. Finally, she threw a stone that actually bounced once before it sank. I think Daddy was more excited than Lindy. He took her up in his arms and danced a little waltz on the sand.

Mama says we have to keep him alive, not just for ourselves, but even more for Lindy. She's afraid Lindy's so young she'll forget him. I don't think that's possible. She might forget what he looked like or the sound of his voice, but I don't think you can forget the feeling of love. I hope not.

I didn't mean for this letter to be so serious. You'll probably never receive it because I won't have the nerve to send it along. If I do, you'll know I was loaded up with too much coffee in the morning and had no idea what I was mailing.

Affectionately,
Eleanor

But she did send it, in a soft pink envelope she found in one of the boxes in the back hall.

Chapter Five

❧ ❧

Robert's letter arrived in the afternoon mail. Mr. Partenope handed it to Eleanor as she sat waiting for him on the bottom step.

"Hot enough for you?" he asked. Sweat dripped from under his cap.

"Too hot," Eleanor said. Too hot to sit out on Mahoney's Point today and read Robert's words. Too many people storms placing their blankets and their picnic baskets — and their toes — on her personal sand.

Mr. Partenope wiped his forehead with a handkerchief. "Seems like you're getting more and more of these letters."

"Seems that way." For once Eleanor didn't try rushing Mr. Partenope along on his way. A knight in shining blue armor, bringing news of the prince to the princess locked in the castle, should be treated with respect and politeness. And right now, Mr. Partenope was her very favorite knight on earth. She practiced her smile. "Hope it cools off for you tomorrow."

"Rain tomorrow. In the nineties again by Saturday."

Eleanor began to get that twitch in her right eye. Being polite and respectful was one thing, but Mr. Partenope acted as if he had all day to stand and talk with her. Not that she minded, not really, but a blue knight should know enough to disappear while the lady of the castle was still smiling at him. "You could have been a weatherman for the radio, Mr. Partenope." She stood and brushed off her skirt with one hand. Robert's letter burned a hole right through the other one. If she could just peek to see if Robert still signed his letter *Affectionately.* Nothing else. But Mr. Partenope didn't move a muscle, and Eleanor was not about to open the letter with him standing right there, his antenna trained on her every move.

"Must be tough on you," she said. "Making all these deliveries in the heat. I suppose the faster you get them over with, the easier it is."

For once, Mr. Paretnope took the hint. "Well, time's a-wasting," he sighed. He heaved the mailbag over his shoulder. "This thing gets heavier every day."

Eleanor didn't say a word. She was too busy counting his steps, revising the number it took him to reach the Beauchamps' triple-decker right next door. There was probably some kind of scientific principle involved, but she had discovered something interesting: the hotter it was, the more steps Mr. Partenope took.

The minute he turned the corner, Eleanor tore open the envelope and checked. There it was. *Affectionately*, just like before. But this time, Robert had added *yours*. She patted the words with the tips of her fingers, then danced them, as if they were miniature ballerinas, across the page. Then she traced Robert's name just once for luck. *Mine!*

June 17, 1944

Dear Eleanor,

You don't always have to entertain me. I'm glad you wrote about your father. The way you talk about him, he must have been a special man.

My parents are special, too, although they always seemed pretty ordinary to me until I enlisted. Mom writes to me every day, and my father types her letters on a banged-up old typewriter he has sitting on his desk in the den. Pop teaches history at the high school in my hometown. He also coaches football. Mom keeps those "home fires burning," along with cooking and sewing and everything else that she does.

When I think of how they had to save every penny to put me through college, well, as I said, my parents are special people. Like yours.

You sound as if you are settling in at your job quite nicely. Clarice and Susan remind me of those comedians Abbott and Costello. Have you figured out which one is which yet? We had a couple of guys here for a short time. Their names were Mick and Mike. None of us knew which was Mick and which was Mike, and they ended up moving on before we ever found out.

Rumors buzz all over the place. It could be a couple of days or a couple of weeks before we ship out. I've had it really good here, so I can't complain. But I always thought I'd get the chance to meet you before I moved on. Perhaps we could meet when this war is over, Eleanor. Where I live in upstate New York is not halfway around the world. We could go to a movie or dancing or just sit on your beach some evening and watch the stars come out. Maybe I'll teach you how to drive a car, and you'll teach me how to skip stones.

Take care of yourself, Eleanor.

Affectionately yours,
Robert

God would punish her if she wished the war would never end, but Eleanor made the wish anyway. Immediately, she crossed herself. "Hail Mary, full of grace," she prayed. What if God decided to punish Robert and not her? What if he actually ended up in Europe or the Pacific, like Mrs. Williams's son? She said another Hail Mary just in case. Every day soldiers suffered horrible injuries, and too many of them died. The papers were filled with news about battles that had never seemed quite real to Eleanor — until now. Even when Mrs. Williams chatted on and on about her Michael this and her Michael that, Eleanor never saw him in her mind the way she saw Robert.

She refolded his letter carefully and placed it in the envelope inside her skirt pocket.

Eleanor didn't remember to retrieve it until after supper, when Mama collected dirty clothes for the wash.

"Another letter from that soldier?" Mama asked when Eleanor grabbed for the envelope.

"I guess it is. I must have forgotten all about it."

"You spend an awful lot of time writing to him, Eleanor. I hear you in the kitchen at night sometimes. I'm not sure that's a good idea."

Eleanor couldn't keep the anger out of her voice. "We're friends. That's all." The muscles in Eleanor's jaw tightened. "He writes about birds and trees and things like that. Things other soldiers aren't interested in."

"Sweetie, you're very young," Mama said. "Your soldier, Robert, might get the wrong idea."

Eleanor saw the worry lines around Mama's mouth. "I don't write to him that often."

But Mama wasn't listening. She had already moved on to another worry. She held up one of Lindy's dresses and sighed. "That sister of yours is growing like a weed. I don't know how long she'll be able to fit into her clothes. Her legs hang out half a mile from the hem, and Mrs. Carvelli has already taken this dress down twice."

Mama should mind her own business when it came to Robert. "You ought to ask Mrs. Carvelli to help."

"Mrs. Carvelli. Mrs. Carvelli. All I hear all day long is Mrs. Carvelli. I'm sorry, Eleanor. But sometimes I feel as if I can't provide for you two girls. You go to work so I can spend some time at home. Lindy spends three days a week with Angela Carvelli. I don't have time to cook for you, to make you a proper meal. I want to give you the things your father would have given you, but I can't. It makes me so angry sometimes." She turned her face away, but not before Eleanor saw tears glistening in Mama's eyes.

All the times in the hospital; all the times Eleanor had awakened, screaming from nightmares about the fire; that first time Eleanor looked in the mirror; the time Mama had packed Daddy's clothes in a box and sent them to St. Mary's Rectory — all those times, Mama hadn't cried once.

Eleanor reached out and grasped her mother's hand. "I like working at the pharmacy. And Lindy, she's like a rubber ball. She bounces. Even if you didn't work, she'd be haunting the Carvellis' apartment. She's just too nosy for words. Just like Mrs. Carvelli. And Mama, about your cooking . . ."

They both laughed. "All right, so maybe it's a good thing I don't spend a lot of time in the kitchen," Mama said.

Lindy bounded through the door. "What are you talking about?" she wanted to know.

"We're talking about you and how we're going to have to put weights on your head so you'll stop growing," Mama said, still smiling.

Lindy put her head up, as if she were the Queen of Sheba, and pursed her lips. "Mr. Carvelli says I am going to be as tall and graceful as a swan when I'm Eleanor's age." She walked around the kitchen, pretending she carried a book on her head. Then Queen Lindy disappeared, and Little Girl Lindy grabbed Mama's arm. "Can Jeannie come over tomorrow to play dolls with me? I want her to meet Cinderella."

Another mouth to feed. Eleanor could read Mama's

expression as clearly as if it were written on her face. "Why don't I bring something home from the drugstore for supper tomorrow," Eleanor said. "Maybe lettuce and tomato sandwiches on toast. Chips, too. To celebrate. Tomorrow I get to cash my very first paycheck."

Except she couldn't cash it, not the way she wanted. She had imagined bringing it to Beachmont Savings and Loan and placing it on the counter in front of the teller. "This is my very first paycheck ever," she would announce to him, and to anyone else who cared to listen. Yes, *this* Eleanor with *this* face actually has a job. But Mrs. Williams took the check out of Eleanor's hands almost before Eleanor read the amount written in blue ink. "Honey, I'll just take this to the register for you and cash it right here. That way you won't have to wander outside in this heat." Eleanor wanted to spit. Rosemary Myers was not the worst pain in Eleanor's existence. The biggest pain was the way everyone in the drugstore treated Eleanor as if she were about to break into a billion pieces. They could have received the Bleeding Heart Award for concern above and beyond the call of duty. Well, except for Rosemary.

"You keep right on working, Eleanor. Customers can wait until I'm not busy anymore," Mr. Carvelli said, waving her back into the cubby when a woman with two children drummed her fingers on the counter.

"Stay where you are, Eleanor. I'll bring your lunch in as soon as the traffic dies down." Mrs. Williams tied a pink apron around her middle. "I'm telling you. These Fridays are killing me," she said, but her words had no bite in them.

On Fridays, half the population of Washington Heights High School planted itself on the soda fountain stools.

Eleanor liked listening to the teenagers chatter. Back and forth the conversations went, like tennis balls across a clay court, interrupted occasionally by roars of laughter. She learned names mostly by voices: Cindy's like a loud, rude crow, Betsy's little-girl trill, Warren's deep bass that rumbled through the store. Once, she snuck a peek around the corner to see if his voice matched his looks. A big, hulking boy with a neck as thick as her waist sat on a stool at the far end of the counter.

"Why do they all come on Fridays?" Eleanor asked.

Mrs. Williams shrugged. "It's a tradition of some kind."

Eleanor repeated the question to Clarice — or was it Susan — when she stopped by the cubby to gather two aprons off the coat rack.

"I think it all started with Michael Williams," the girl explained. "He used to work the fountain every Friday. He was really popular." She smiled a little to herself. "And he was nice, too — even to younger kids like me. His friends used to come down to see him at lunchtime. When he went away, well, I think now everyone comes down to be with Mrs. Williams instead. So she won't be so lonely without him." She hugged the aprons to her chest. "I have to get going now, Eleanor," she said as she started out the door. Then she paused. "Do you need anything? Tonic maybe? Chips?"

Another Bleeding Heart recipient. "I don't need anything. But thank you for asking," Eleanor answered. She picked up a prescription and held it in front of her face. "I had better get back to work myself."

But she couldn't concentrate. Clarice and Susan were whispering in the bathroom. She didn't mean to listen. But their conversation was so close. Besides, they had mentioned her name.

"It's so hard sometimes. Not that I can't stand the sight of her or anything. It's just that I keep thinking how much it must have hurt. Do you think it still does? Hurt Eleanor, I mean?" Was that Clarice, with the squeaky voice and hesitant *d's*?

The other voice didn't squeak. "Why don't you just ask her?"

"I can't do that. I wouldn't want to hurt her feelings. People are always staring at her. And you know how rude Rosemary is. I heard her say that Eleanor should wear make-up to hide her scars. It's so unfair, too, because pieces of her face are still pretty. We're not like Rosemary, are we? We try to be nice."

"We're just fine," the other voice agreed. "We treat her real nice, like Mrs. Williams and Mr. Carvelli do."

Stop it! Eleanor wanted to scream at them. *I don't want to be treated "nice." I want you to tease me and get angry with me and hurt my feelings because you forgot to be careful. Like you do with your friends sitting out there.*

But wasn't she just as bad, the way she avoided the soda fountain and the customers? Eleanor stared at the blotter with *RB* printed in each corner. She couldn't hide in a cubby her whole life long. She waited until she couldn't hear the girls' voices anymore.

"I'm thirsty," she told Mr. Carvelli. "I'm going to get some tonic, or a Coca-Cola maybe."

Mr. Carvelli had prescriptions stacked an inch high on his counter. "I'll get you one in a little while, Eleanor. Or maybe one of the girls" — he never could remember their names — "will get you what you want."

"No, Mr. Carvelli. I'll get it myself."

She stepped out from the back room and pushed her way through the crowd at the fountain. Mrs. Williams must have been somewhere, Rosemary, too, but the only person Eleanor saw was the taller of the two girls. She stood behind the counter, filling two glasses with orange tonic. Eleanor ignored her. She took a glass from the back shelf and placed it under the Coca-Cola dispenser. She could hear every tick of her watch, every beat of her heart.

"I don't know how to work this!" She said the words out loud.

"Clarice, you want to help Eleanor with that?" Mrs. Williams called out. The girl started to take the glass, but Eleanor held onto it. "I can do it if you show me how."

Never again would she confuse Clarice with Susan. Clarice was the one with the kind eyes. "Push the handle. Don't pull it," Clarice said. Her shoulder bumped against Eleanor's as she moved away from the tonic machine. "It's not hard. You'll be fine."

"Thank you." With trembling hands, Eleanor pushed and watched the brown liquid swirl into her glass. She took one sip, then another. Over the rim of her glass, she checked the soda fountain crowd.

Mrs. Williams chattered away while she flipped grilled

cheese sandwiches on the grill. Susan flirted with a pimple-faced boy with black glasses and an Adam's apple that bobbed up and down every time he swallowed. At the far end of the counter, Rosemary primped and strutted for a policeman sipping his cup of coffee. *Lord. You'd hope a policeman would have better taste than to pay attention to someone like Rosemary.*

A couple of the boys glanced her way. One girl let her sandwich fall back onto her plate before she turned quickly toward the boy beside her. But nobody bolted from their seat. Nobody pointed a finger at her or stared.

These weak knees and shaking hands were all for nothing? She leaned against the wall as she sipped her Coke. Mrs. Williams pushed a plate with a sandwich and chips into Eleanor's hand. "Here, young lady. Eat up. You're too skinny by half. But first I want you to meet someone." She planted her hands on the pimply boy's shoulders. "Eleanor, this is Tony, my Michael's best friend in the world. Tony here has been hanging around my kitchen since he and Michael were in the first grade. That's fourteen years now and counting." Tony's ears turned as red as Rosemary's nail polish. He had to be almost twenty, but he looked so much younger with those red cheeks and his uncertain smile. Eleanor felt decades older than he looked.

"Hey! Mrs. W.! Speaking of that boy of yours, you hear anything from Michael lately?" The policeman had a huge voice that interrupted everyone's chatter.

"I'm telling you, Ed. I've been saving my sugar ration all month just to make gingersnaps. I even got a salami from Bailey's. But I'm not sure I like those Marines very much. They wouldn't let me send anything until Michael finished basic training. He got in trouble when I mailed him a package before. They took it away from him. Then they made him do I-don't-know-how-many push-ups. That's not a very nice thing to do to a growing boy."

Eleanor was positive Ed was looking at her when he winked. "They just want their boys to be real tough for the fighting."

"My Michael is tough enough already," Mrs. Williams said wistfully. "I don't want him to turn into one of those big, loudmouthed soldiers who swill beer and get into fistfights."

"Don't you worry your head, Mrs. W., I'm sure they tucked him in every night of basic training and fed him his milk and cookies."

Mrs. Williams reached across the counter and swatted Ed with a towel. "Get on with you now. Don't you have some criminal to catch somewhere?"

They sounded so comfortable with each other. Somewhere in upstate New York someone, perhaps his father, was teasing Robert's mother the same way. She would look like Mrs. Williams a little, too, and say the same type of things. *Get on with you now. Don't you have a team to coach somewhere?*

Mama didn't understand at all. Eleanor didn't write to Robert just because she liked him. Of course she liked him, but he needed her to keep his spirits up, too. That's what you did for soldiers. You sent them letters or packages of cookies and books so they wouldn't feel so lonely.

Eleanor finished her sandwich and placed the dish by the sink. Tonight, no matter what Mama said, Eleanor was sending another letter.

June 20, 1944

Dear Robert,

Mrs. Williams taught me how to work the register this afternoon. Believe me, this is an honor greater than winning a Nobel Prize. I don't think Mrs. Williams even trusts Mr. Carvelli when it comes to money. "You put the twenties under the drawer," she's always reminding him. But right before she left, she counted everything. "It balances right to the penny," she announced to everyone in the store. "You'd make a great accountant." I have to tell you, though. The thought of sitting behind a desk adding and subtracting numbers all day long is not my idea of a career with great potential.

I'm glad you don't mind me writing about my father. People are afraid to mention his name, afraid my mother or I or Lindy will break into pieces if they do. I'm not quite sure how to explain this. I want them to remember him, because that way he can't really be dead.

My father was tall with gray hair and a bald spot right in the middle of his head. He had huge hands. You would think they'd be too big to do much of anything with them, but he could sew the smallest stitches and tie the tiniest knots. Daddy was a general practitioner. He worked too hard, and he loved books and dogs.

I miss him a lot. I miss the way he whistled when he was raking the grass. Actually, this is going to sound really strange, but I miss grass. You know how it smells when you just cut it? Beachmont doesn't have a lot of green anything, at least not where we live. I miss the lilac bush out back and the glider on our back porch. But at least I still have the ocean. When it's too rainy or cool for people to go swimming, the beach is deserted. That's my favorite time. I walk along the edge of the water and pick up shells like I did when I was a little kid.

I shouldn't be talking about missing things when I'm the one who is home safe with my family and you're the one so far away from yours. I really hope you don't go overseas, Robert. I hope you stay here until Germany and Japan surrender.

Stay safe.

Affectionately yours,
Eleanor

Chapter Six

❦ ❧

June 22, 1944

*D*ear Eleanor,

For the first time since I've been here, the dorm is silent. All the guys are taking advantage of the weather and the day to have one final fling before orders come. I'm a little tired of New York. In my hometown, the highlight of a Sunday afternoon is sitting on the porch, counting the cars that drive by. I'm exaggerating a little. Townshend is quiet, though. I like that. Lots of trees line the streets, and houses have wide porches and windowboxes in the summer.

Look at me, saying all this to a city girl. But the way you love empty beaches more than full ones makes me think you understand.

I know what you mean when you write about missing grass. It doesn't sound silly at all. I miss my dog. She's part Airedale and part sheep dog and who knows what else. Her name is Snowball, but my friends call her the Dust Mop, and she does look like one. We've had her since I was nine years old. Every night, she used to follow me into my bedroom and throw herself down on the floor beside my bed. Every morning when the alarm went off, I would have to push her out of the way with my feet. "It's morning, Snowball. Time to get up. Come on, move." At least that's how it used to be before the war interrupted everything. I miss her and the way the floor was always warm where she slept.

How ironic life is. When I was young, I couldn't wait to leave home and go off into the world, searching for adventure. Now, all I want to do is go back to Townshend for one day, even for one hour.

I feel like a little kid spending the summer at camp for the first time.

Please take care of yourself, Eleanor.

Affectionately yours,
Robert

Eleanor could picture him rubbing the dog's stomach with his toes. *Snowball.* She would bet a million dollars that Robert named the dog himself. She imagined him as a tousled, mud-covered nine-year-old, holding a wriggling bundle of fur in his arms and announcing to his parents, "Her name is Snowball." It was like she owned a secret piece of Robert now, a piece she could take out whenever she needed to feel that she was special to someone. And she *was* special to him. Not like the other girls he knew. *Other girls.* Robert must have known a lot of them. Girls would fall all over someone like Robert. But none of them knew those pieces he kept hidden from everyone but her.

Mrs. Williams stepped into the back room — everyone called it "Eleanor's cubby" now — and Eleanor shoved Robert's letter into her pocket.

"Eleanor, would you watch the register for a few minutes? I have to change the oil in the fryers. It's supposed to be Rosemary's job but . . . well, at least it'll be done right this time."

Eleanor grabbed a handful of prescriptions and cards and headed for the counter. Mr. Carvelli smiled as she straightened the vitamin display by the cash register. "Mrs. Williams and me — I — we are always saying how lucky we are that we found you, Eleanor. Such a good worker. And trustworthy."

Eleanor knew exactly why Lindy's feet couldn't quite contain her happiness sometimes, because Eleanor's own toes bounced inside her shoes. "Thank you, Mr. Carvelli. But I'm the lucky one."

She concentrated so hard on the prescription cards that she didn't realize a customer was standing in front of her until he cleared his throat. Eleanor raised her head. *Don't forget to smile. It's good for you. Stretches those cheek muscles.* The man was smiling back at her, a lopsided grin that made him look boyish. He had nice eyes, too. They were blue, and they crinkled at the edges as if he had spent too much time squinting into the sun.

"May I help you with something?"

He placed a bottle of aspirin on the counter. "My wife," he said. "She's always getting headaches."

He reached into his pocket and removed a five-dollar bill.

He lay the money on the counter and rested his hands on either side of it. Eleanor picked up a bag from under the counter and placed the aspirin inside. She didn't look at the bag. She didn't touch the money. She didn't even look up. Because of the man's hands. His poor, scarred hands.

They had ridges and bumps. Candle-wax skin covered them and melted right down to his fingertips. She tried to look away, tried to concentrate on the cash register instead. *Place the five on the ledge in front of the drawer, Eleanor. Press "Open." Find the four dollars and sixty-three cents change. Count the money into those hands. Whatever you do, though, don't stare at those hands.*

Those hands!

The man cleared his throat again. "Miss?"

"Yes?"

"Do you mind me asking? I mean, it's not my business or anything, but if you don't mind me asking . . ."

He waited for a moment, then finished his question. "You're a mite young, but I was just wondering. It wasn't the Palm Gardens fire, was it? Your face, I mean? Meaning no disrespect."

Eleanor's heart beat so loudly she knew everyone could hear it. The part of her mind that still functioned looked out at Carvelli's middle aisle, at boxes of heating pads near the top shelf. *Mrs. Williams will have a fit if she notices how dusty they are. I'll take care of them so Clarice and Susan don't get in trouble later.*

Her mind froze on the word *later.* Later — after this person with his terrible hands left the drugstore.

"Miss?" the man said.

Eleanor's hand reached for her cheek and she nodded.

The pictures she had hidden away for months came back to her in flashes like bolts of lightning: the sudden gasp from a hundred people as the whole back of the room lit up with flames, Daddy holding her with an iron grip, Daddy pulling her through the crowd. And always, through everything, that awful smell of burning.

"Miss? Miss, are you OK?"

The images disappeared, but the smell of burned meat remained, leaving Eleanor trembling and fearful.

"It's the smell," she said weakly.

Mr. Carvelli called out sharply. "Eleanor? When you finish with your customer, I need a bottle of pills from the back."

The man turned to leave but paused for a moment. "I'm sorry. I didn't mean to upset you. I shouldn't have mentioned the fire that way. It's just so rare seeing someone else who was there. Someone who knows."

Mr. Carvelli waited in the back room for her, his face sweating concern. "Are you all right, Eleanor? I don't mean to speak like that to you. I just thought maybe you wanted to get away and not talk about the fire anymore with that man."

His eyes reminded her so much of Daddy's eyes — soft and brown, and concerned — that she had to turn toward the backroom to hide her tears. She couldn't fall apart right now and break the heart of this kind little man.

For the rest of the afternoon, Eleanor hid in her cubby. Mrs. Williams walked through a few times. Once she asked, "How's your stomach holding up, honey? Ready for some food yet?" She placed her hand on Eleanor's head. The warmth of that hand made Eleanor's throat tighten. She shook her head, and Mrs. Williams left her alone again.

For a long time after that, Eleanor stared at the remaining stack of prescriptions. Her fingers traced the lettering on the corners of the blotter, memorizing the curve of each initial. In the middle drawer of the desk, she found a pad of paper and a pencil.

June 27, 1944

Dear Robert,

I really shouldn't be writing this to you now because I'm at work, and I feel as if I'm cheating Mr. Carvelli. But I haven't eaten anything all day, so I'll count this as my lunch hour instead.

A man came into the store this afternoon. I waited on him. He had really horrible scars, as if he had been in a fire. It was hard to look at him. I don't mean he disgusted me, but he made me think about what his life must be like.

I worry sometimes, when I see people like that. How do they get up each morning, knowing that the whole day long, people are going to stare at them or be disgusted by them or just plain pity them? I wonder if anyone ever sees them as real people with feelings that get hurt? Does he have a wife who can forget his scars and love him anyway?

I'm sorry. It's just that — Daddy's gone, and if I tell my mother what I worry about, she'll want to pour cod liver oil down my throat. That's Mama's solution for anything that ails you. And Lindy's too young to understand. My friends and I haven't spent much time together since I moved here.

*Beachmont is only twenty miles from Cape Ann, but it might
as well be in California.*

*I promise, the next time I write, I will be my "bright and
funny" self — your words, not mine, remember.*

Please stay safe.

Affectionately yours,
Eleanor

On the way home from work, she dropped the letter into
the mailbox by her streetcar stop. It would take her letter two
days to reach New York. That meant in two days Robert would
read what she had written. Maybe it would take a day for him
to answer. That left two days for his letter to reach her. Five
days, six at the most, and she would know. She had to know.
She touched her cheek with her fingers. If he understood how
she felt about the man with the burned hands, he just might
understand about her face.

Two blond heads bobbed up and down as Lindy and
another little girl leaned their backs against the front porch
rail. Eleanor stopped on the bottom step and listened to
General Lindy giving orders to her troop of one. "I'm the
princess 'cause Cinderella, she's a princess in disguise, you
see. That's why she gets the prince in the end. Your doll can be
her sister — Bertina."

The other little girl began to protest, but Lindy cut her off.
"It's not me, Jearnie. It's the way the story goes."

So this was Jeannie — finally. Eleanor had to bite the
inside of her cheek to keep from laughing out loud. Lindy had

been so disappointed yesterday when Jeannie called to say she couldn't come over. Now Eleanor wondered. Maybe Lindy's bossiness had something to do with the cancellation. But then, Eleanor had once been just as bossy. Her Nancy Ann doll had ruled the yard from beneath Mama's peonies the same way Cinderella ruled the Carvellis' front porch. Yet every afternoon, Marybeth had arrived with her trunk of clothes and furniture in one hand and her Jeff doll dangling from the other.

How lucky Lindy was to have found someone, the way she had found Marybeth.

Jeannie stood abruptly. "What time is it? I have to know the time." Her eyes were searchlights, scanning the sky, the street, and finally the porch steps. They stopped when they reached Eleanor's face. Jeannie stumbled. Her fingers reached for the porch railing. She stammered words that Eleanor couldn't understand, then burst into tears.

Lindy panicked. "Jeannie, what's wrong? Jeannie, your doll is a princess, just like Cinderella. And she'll go to the ball. The fairy godmother will take her, too."

Eleanor hurried up the steps, two at a time. In her gentlest voice, she said, "What's the matter, honey? Did you hurt yourself? Did something frighten you?" She tried to pat Jeannie's shoulder, but the little girl shrank away as if Eleanor had slapped her.

"Don't you touch me!" she screamed. "Mommy! I want my Mommy!"

"Eleanor! You're here." Tears had already begun to form in Lindy's eyes. "Do something, Ellie. Jeannie's crying. Did you hurt yourself, Jeannie? My sister Eleanor's here. She can fix you up good."

Eleanor's hand dropped to her side. She stepped back. "I can't fix Jeannie. She's not hurt," Eleanor said. "It's my fault. Your friend is crying because she's afraid of me, Lindy."

It's all right, Jeannie. You don't have to be afraid. I'm Eleanor, and I was in a bad fire. That's all. It's okay, honey. That's the kind of thing the man with the burned hands would have said. But Eleanor couldn't say the words. She pushed past Lindy, past Jeannie, through the front door, and up the stairs to the apartment. She wiped her eyes with the palms of her hands because she had to be crying. That's what people did when life was this cruel. They cried. But her hands were dry when she pulled them from her face.

Eleanor headed straight into the bedroom. She dropped to her knees and pulled the shoebox out from under the bed. And she stayed there, kneeling, while she took Robert's letters, one by one, from the box.

Dear Eleanor . . . I enjoy your letters . . . Affectionately . . . You're smart and you understand people's feelings . . . Don't mean to play the big brother . . . Take care of yourself, Eleanor . . . Affectionately yours.

She held the letters to her cheek, feeling their coolness against her skin. Here, in Robert's letters, was her only safe place. No storms could threaten her, no little girl's tears could hurt her. In this little world where just she and Robert lived, nothing mattered except what she thought and felt and wrote with Daddy's fountain pen.

Mama sat down on the floor next to Eleanor but didn't hug

her. Eleanor was glad. She hurt too much, as if all the cruel things people had ever said to her had bruised her skin and made it too tender to be touched. She hid her head inside her shoulders and wrapped her arms around her knees.

"Eleanor."

"I don't want to talk about it, Mama."

"Lindy told me what happened. She is so worried — about you."

"I don't want to talk about it."

"Sweetie . . ."

"It doesn't matter anyway."

"It matters, Eleanor. When you were a little girl, I could take you in my arms and heal all the hurts." Mama stroked Eleanor's hair. She played with it, twisting the ends around her fingers the way she had when Eleanor was six and had begged for Shirley Temple curls.

The words burst out of Eleanor's mouth like bombs exploding into the sky. "When I was a little girl, I had a father and a face. If I could have one, just *one* of them now. Daddy . . ." She couldn't continue. The words hurt too much to say. *Daddy didn't save my life. He ruined it.*

She allowed Mama's arms to come around her and hug her close. She even rested her head against Mama's chest and felt the steady rhythm of Mama's heartbeat. But no tears came.

Lindy wore a faded pink nightgown with lace trim and sat on the edge of Eleanor's bed. "Are you still mad?" she asked. Her fingers played with the top sheet, folding it into little accordion pleats.

Eleanor lay flat across the bed. She wore blue pajamas with no trim. "I was never angry, Lindy."

"I'm sorry, Ellie."

"It's all right, Lindy. Everything is fine. I'm fine. Go to sleep now." She turned on her side and buried her face against the pillow.

"Jeannie's sorry, too. I know she is."

"Please, Lindy. Just go to sleep."

"Do you want to keep Cinderella for tonight?"

Eleanor didn't answer. She waited until Lindy returned to her own bed before she allowed herself to cry. Then the tears that had bottled up in her throat all day escaped and spilled onto her pillow.

Chapter Seven

ல ை

Mr. Carvelli poked his head inside the cubby. "Elcanor, do you have Mr. Mackey's record card? David Mackey? I need to see his most recent medicines."

"It's here somewhere. Just let me look for a minute." Eleanor pushed aside the grilled cheese sandwich she had been eating and attacked the pile of customer cards instead.

"Don't bother. I'll call Dr. Fredericks to find out," Mr. Carvelli said.

"No! Wait. I can find it. It has to be here someplace."

But Mr. Carvelli's head had already disappeared.

Eleanor gulped down the rest of her sandwich. Four bites. Record speed. All morning long, she had waited on customers, even though Mrs. Williams was perfectly capable of doing that. She dusted the back shelves, even though Clarice had wiped them down just yesterday. But she had not picked up one prescription and copied it onto one customer card.

Until now. *That's it. No more dawdling.* In her best handwriting, Eleanor began copying the doctor's words. Marion Thomas. June 15, 1944. Sulfur, 400 mg. Dr. Louis Mazer. Or was that Glazer? No wonder she put off this horrible job. Figuring out which doctor wrote what instructions to which patient made her head ache.

Eleanor paused. *I need your letter, Robert. Now!* Yesterday, she had hoped his letter would be there. She had held the same hope the day before — and the day before that. Every afternoon this week, she had hurried home and sorted the mail into little piles, hoping somehow Robert's letter had attached itself to another one. And every afternoon, her hope had melted into a puddle of disappointment.

The pencil slipped out of Eleanor's fingers. No maybe about it. Robert's answer was waiting for her today. Eleanor knew absolutely. She could picture the red and blue border, that black writing, the curve of that *E.*

Time stood still. That's what she used to think during sophomore year, sitting through Sister Eloise Mary's world history class. Every afternoon, Sister droned on and on about the essential by-products of iron ore and other boring subjects. And every afternoon, Eleanor drew daisies in the margins of her notebook paper or wrote notes to Marybeth. "Let's count how many times Sister Lulu May says 'okay' in the next ten minutes."

But waiting for the hands of Carvelli's clock to move even a fraction of an inch toward five o'clock was much worse than listening to Sister Eloise. Three times in a row, she wrote *Robert Bettencourt* instead of the actual doctor's name, and three times in a row she had to tear the card into tiny pieces so Nosy Miss Rosemary wouldn't see Eleanor's mistake. The woman noticed absolutely everything. "Bring your lunch today, did you?" she asked. She inspected the waxpaper in the wastebasket before plopping into the chair opposite Eleanor. Her voice reminded Eleanor of fingernails scraping against a chalkboard. "Tired of Mrs. Williams's cooking?"

"Chocolate chip cookies. From Mrs. Williams." Eleanor patted her stomach. "Best cookies in the world."

"Hmm. Seems like some people around here get special treatment."

Eleanor nodded. "Some people do, I guess."

Mrs. Williams called out as she stocked the shelves behind the soda fountain. "Rosemary, did you get that dust mop for me yet, the way I asked you to? It's right behind Eleanor's desk there. The blue handle."

The thick layer of powder Rosemary wore on her face couldn't hide her red cheeks. "As if I never saw a dust mop in my entire life!" she sputtered. She didn't say thank you when Eleanor handed the mop to her.

Eleanor waited until Rosemary disappeared behind the counter. Then she took a pencil and wrote "The Mouth" in huge block letters across the blotter page.

She hid the word with her hand when Mrs. Williams pushed through the doorway to place her apron on the coat rack. "We have to do something about these girls," Mrs. Williams announced.

"Mrs. Williams?"

"Twenty-three cents. That's what the cash register was off when I checked before we opened this morning. Forty-eight cents the day before. Don't they teach math in those schools anymore?" Then she got that soft, my-baby-boy look in her eyes. "Course, I shouldn't complain so much. My Michael wasn't too good with money, either. Always forgetting what he did with it. I'd have to peel the money out of Michael's pockets when he finished deliveries. 'I think I put it in this pocket, Ma. No? Well, let me check this one.'"

Eleanor drummed her fingers along the edge of the desk. What did she care about twenty-three missing cents?

"Are you all right, Eleanor?" Mrs. Williams asked. She peered into Eleanor's face as if she were searching for symptoms of tuberculosis or worse.

"I'm fine. I'm just fine," Eleanor said. She remembered saying the same words to Dr. Gilligan before he released her into Mama's care.

"I know a doctor," Dr. Gilligan had said. "James Chamberlain. You might like to talk with him. He's not a doctor the way I am. He heals people's minds."

"I don't need to talk to anyone like that."

"Other people — from the fire — and soldiers hurt in the war — they found him helpful."

"But I don't *need* help. I'm fine. I'm just fine."

She didn't need any Dr. Chamberlain telling her that she could learn to live with her face.

Right now, she didn't need to listen to Clarice and Susan standing at the front of the store, twittering away like sparrows.

They had arrived together, as usual, bounding through the door, laughing the whole time. Their laughter hurt her ears.

Susan waited in the cubby doorway while Clarice gathered the packages to be delivered from the shelf above Eleanor's head. "I can't believe you got him to go with us," Clarice said.

Susan smiled. "I have my ways." They both giggled again.

Eleanor slapped a prescription onto the desk so hard her palm stung.

"Is everything all right?" Clarice wanted to know.

"Everything is just fine."

"We're going to the movies tomorrow night with Tony," Clarice said. She ignored Susan's sigh. "Do you want to come with us?"

"No, thank you. I'm busy," Eleanor said. *Miss Priss.* That's what John Belleveau had once called Eleanor. "Miss Priss could freeze you to death with her attitude."

She was being Miss Priss right now, and she didn't care.

Susan flounced out of the cubby.

"Please, Eleanor, is anything wrong? Are you mad at me for something?"

"I'm fine," Eleanor answered.

"Then come with us." Clarice abandoned the packages in her hand. Just like Lindy begging to play dolls, she grabbed Eleanor's arm and shook it gently. "Please? It'll be just us — we can sit together in the theater and let Susan be with Tony."

"I have to check with my mother. See if she made plans for tomorrow."

Clarice pushed the chair back from the desk and stood. "It's all right. I understand."

"I didn't say I wouldn't go. It's just — I have other things on my mind right now."

"So go to the movies with us and take your mind off of them."

Eleanor shuffled the prescription cards. She picked up a pencil and drew another daisy in each corner of the blotter paper. What if Robert wanted to visit Beachmont someday? After she wrote to him and told him the truth. After he wrote back, "You will always be beautiful to me, ocean girl." He would want to go places — to the movie theater, maybe. He wouldn't want to just sit on the porch and listen to Mrs. Carvelli's words of wisdom.

"Let me check with my mother, Clarice."

Clarice clapped her hands. "She'll say yes. I know she'll say yes."

No envelopes lay on the front hall table. Eleanor rested her hand on the polished surface. Robert's letter *had* to be here. She checked the floor underneath the table, the space between the table and the wall. No mail. No envelopes. Nothing.

That meant Mama had picked up the mail. Or Lindy.

"If you're looking for something to eat, there are crackers by the sink," Mama said the moment Eleanor walked through the kitchen door. Mama and Lindy sat at the table, their heads bent over sheets of paper dolls.

"I cut off her head by accident," Lindy wailed.

Mama inspected the doll. "That's why God invented tape," she said. "Nurses make pretty good surgeons, if I do say so myself."

The click of scissors scraped Eleanor's nerves raw.

"I'm going to my room," she announced. She paused. "I don't suppose anything interesting came in the mail today. Not that anything interesting ever does."

"Bills and more bills. A letter from the Currens. You received a letter, too. It's on your bed."

"It's from Robert!" Lindy said. She wore a triumphant look, as if the letter belonged to her instead of Eleanor.

Mama tightened her mouth. "Little sisters should learn to mind their own business," she said. But she hadn't quite perfected Sister Agnes's "hairy eyeball" look. "Eleanor, we'll be eating supper around six. Spaghetti and meatballs. Angela sent them up."

Eleanor stood in front of her bedroom door. Her hand rested on the knob, but she didn't turn it. Her breath came in huge gulps, as if she had run home all the way from the drugstore. *Please, Robert.* The words helped her open the door and walk into the room.

Robert's letter lay in the middle of Eleanor's bed. She sat next to it with hands folded on her lap. From the kitchen, she could hear Lindy's squeaky chattering, interrupted once in a while by Mama's deeper tones. She counted to ten, as if she were waiting for Mr. Partenope. Then she counted to ten again. Her hands brushed the chenille bedspread. She picked up the envelope and turned it over. Her fingers trembled when she finally lifted the flap and pulled out the tissue-thin pages.

June 29, 1944

Dear Eleanor,

I promise not to feed you cod liver oil no matter what you write.

Actually, I'm glad you feel comfortable enough with me to tell me what's really on your mind.

You are a very sensitive girl, but worrying about the feelings of a complete stranger will drive you crazy. The man you saw at the drugstore probably doesn't even think about how ugly he is. That's what usually happens. Something bad happens to us, and we get on with our lives.

I wish I had more time to write, but I have an exam in French to practice for. My mother would keel over if she knew what words were going to be in the vocabulary section. I promise to write again soon.

Please take care of yourself, Eleanor. I wouldn't want anything bad to happen to you.

> *Affectionately yours,*
> *Robert*

I wouldn't want anything bad to happen to you? Eleanor laughed. *Too late, Robert. A year and a half too late.* She brushed her hand against the smooth side of her face. "Pieces of her face are still pretty," Clarice had said to Susan. But Robert wasn't Clarice. Robert would never see those pieces. Eleanor knew that now. *Ugly!* Why did she ever think he would understand? How could she ever have imagined that he would see the real Eleanor?

She tried to shred the letter, but her fingers slid off its edges. *Ugly!* She couldn't say the word out loud, because it would become a never-ending scream. Mama would hear. And Lindy's eyes would widen and her little face crumple, the way it had the other day when Jeannie was so upset.

Pretend, Eleanor. Pretend that everything is fine. Go into the kitchen just before suppertime as if "ugly" isn't crushing your chest.

But pretending was impossible. The minute she walked into the kitchen, Lindy asked, "Eleanor, will you play dolls with me? I didn't have anyone to play dolls with today."

"You have friends in every house and every apartment on this block," Eleanor hissed. "Why do you need to bother me?"

Mama said, "You don't mind watching your sister after supper while I run down to the store for some bread and milk, do you?"

"What would you do if I said I minded?" Eleanor muttered under her breath. They were picking her skin apart at the seams.

That night, Eleanor waited until Mama closed her own bedroom door and Lindy's eyes closed in sleep. Then she walked into the kitchen and sat at the table.

July 5, 1944

Dear Robert,

Your last letter surprised me. I probably am very sensitive, as you say. But I don't think that people who have been burned are "ugly." I think ugliness depends on who you are inside.

I'm telling you this because I know exactly how the burned

man feels. Maybe I know even better. You see, I was burned in
a fire, too. My face is "ugly" now. Except pieces of it.

Eleanor's hands shook too much to continue. She couldn't
see the words or the paper or the table or the kitchen itself.
And she didn't even know that Lindy was kneeling on the
floor beside her until Lindy's arm came around her shoulders.

"Are you crying because of Daddy?" Lindy's face twisted
with concern. "I do that sometimes. When no one sees me. I
cry because I don't want Daddy to be gone."

Eleanor shoved the half-written letter into her pocket. "It's
not because of Daddy, Lindy. Sometimes I just have to cry.
Just because."

"Is it because your face hurts you? Jeannie asked me if
your face hurt you."

"My face doesn't hurt, Lindy. I'm fine. You don't have to
worry about me."

"I bet Robert worries about you too, huh, Ellie?"

The muscles around Eleanor's mouth tightened, as if she
were protecting herself from the pain of a toothache. "He has
a lot on his mind, Lindy. With the war and everything."

Lindy curled into Eleanor's body. She leaned her head
against Eleanor's chest.

"I like Robert. He's nice. I told Jeannie about him. Is that
all right? Because she thinks her sister is so special, just
because she's engaged and everything."

Lindy and her fantasy world. Eleanor threaded her
fingers through Lindy's hair, stroking the soft curls. Too bad
that world didn't exist. A fairy godmother or two might be
nice. Cindereleanor, maybe. A fairy godmother could make

her so beautiful that the prince would fall in love with her on sight. And they would live happily ever after. Except now the prince would never be Robert.

Ugly! Even while she unpacked Purington's drug order and placed the bottles of pills on shelves in the back room, the word kept pounding into Eleanor's brain. She couldn't push it away; she couldn't rip it into tiny pieces and throw it into the wastebasket.

Clarice stood in the doorway, her shoulder leaning against its frame. "So what did your mother say?"

Her voice startled Eleanor. "What did my mother say about what?"

"About going to the movies." Clarice held the delivery packages in one hand while she picked at the buttons on her blouse with the other. "It really would be a lot of fun. And it would help me a lot. All Susan wants to do is make googly eyes at Tony, and I feel funny being there alone with them. Like I'm in the way."

Eleanor could have touched the hurt in Clarice's voice. She had heard that hurt before — in Marybeth's voice the time Eleanor bubbled all over the place about Jack Carmody asking her to the movies. "That's really great, Eleanor. I'm really happy for you," Marybeth had said. But she sounded as if she were pretending.

Eleanor had pretended, too, that she hadn't heard Marybeth's unhappiness. After all, they had both liked the same boy before. Sometimes Marybeth ended up with him; sometimes Eleanor did. Their competition was just a game.

It hadn't occurred to Eleanor until now that in every game, there has to be a loser.

"Sure. I'll go. Why not?" Eleanor said.

"We really will have the best time. I promise. I'll tell Susan."

Eleanor drew a big *X* over the prescription card in front of her. "I'm not sure Susan will want me there."

"Oh, don't mind her. She's just jealous."

"Jealous? Of me?"

"Tony asks us about you sometimes. Asks if we know where you go to school and where you moved here from."

The cubby suddenly became stifling hot. "If he's so curious, he should just ask me."

"Oh, he's not being mean. He's really nice. He's just making conversation."

But Eleanor could feel the steam building inside her, like a pressure cooker about to explode. *Nosy boy. Who does he think he is, asking questions about me as if I'm some sort of science experiment?* He made her nervous sometimes, the way he watched her, that soft voice of his.

But Clarice was so eager. And she had been very kind.

"You need to tell me when to meet you."

"I'll check," Clarice said. "Right now, I'd better be getting back to work before Mrs. Williams has my head."

But Mrs. Williams wasn't having anyone's head. She didn't even check the cash register drawer when Susan shoved handfuls of money inside it after the deliveries. Instead, she puttered around, moving the Pepto Bismol bottles from one shelf to another, pushing the boxes in beside the cough drops. Then she moved the bottles back. She said nothing about dusting or sweeping. She didn't even complain when the register was off by almost a dollar.

"There's lots of fighting going on in the Pacific. That's where her son is. Lots of casualties," Clarice whispered to Eleanor on her way out of the cubby.

Eleanor's stomach turned right over. She didn't want to think about fighting, about war, about men dying. Every time she did, a chill came over her body. Even now, in the heat of the drugstore, the skin on her fingers tightened with cold. Dr. Gilligan had said, "You'll have to be more careful now, Eleanor. Scars make you vulnerable. They don't do a very good job of regulating your temperature, so you're liable to feel chilled, even on the hottest days." But Eleanor knew better. Scar tissue wasn't what made her cold. Fear did that.

And she couldn't help being afraid for Robert. Even now. Even though he wasn't *Robert, Robert, Robert* anymore, but just another one of those people storms raging around her.

Chapter Eight

❧ ❧

Eleanor had no brains. That's what she decided as she stood in front of Mama's dresser, while Mama pulled the hair from Eleanor's face and caught it in a blue ribbon she had borrowed from one of Cinderella's dresses. If Eleanor really *did* have a brain in her head, she would not be going through this torture, not even for Clarice and her kind heart.

"I'm so glad you are going out with your friends," Mama was saying.

Eleanor spoke through clenched teeth. "I don't know about this, Mama."

"Well, I do. Your hair looks beautiful this way." Mama broke sprigs of baby's breath from the vase on her dresser and wove them through the ribbon with expert fingers. "It curls under perfectly. I can never get mine to behave like that. Loose ends start popping out all over the place."

"I'm afraid to move a muscle. If I move my head, my hair

will come undone. If I move any other part of me, my dress will wrinkle."

Mama laughed. "Sweetie, it's okay to relax. Nothing is going to come apart. I used to worry, too. When we were first dating, Daddy used to tease me all the time. 'Sometimes I feel like I'm going out with one of those mannequins from Jordan Marsh.'"

Lindy burrowed under discarded dresses and hair nets. "You look pretty, Ellie," she said from her clothing cavern.

The word is ugly, *Lindy.* Eleanor gripped the edge of the bureau with both hands. *Think about Clarice. Think how disappointed she'll be if you chicken out now.*

"I hate the way they're always changing styles on us," Mama sighed. "One year, long skirts are popular. The very next spring, hems stop at your knees. I doubt it has anything to do with the war effort."

"You could shorten this dress, Mama," Eleanor said. "Then you could wear it again yourself."

Mama raised her eyebrows. Thread and Mama didn't mix. She used to pay Dell's Cleaners to sew all the missing buttons on Daddy's shirts.

"No. You wear it. You're tall enough. The length's just perfect for you."

Eleanor checked. She bent from side to side, inspecting her legs, making sure their paleness didn't contrast too much with the dark blue cotton. The skirt swung every time she moved. She used to like that swish of fabric against her legs.

Lindy dug her way out of the cave. "Doesn't she look pretty, Mama?"

Mama kissed Eleanor's cheek. "You do look good, sweetie. Blue is definitely your color. Brings out the color in your eyes."

After Mama shooed Lindy into the kitchen, Eleanor stood in front of Mama's dresser. The mirror taunted her. *Look. Just once. One fast look.*

She stroked her scarred cheek. Could the skin be less puckery? Maybe Dr. Gilligan was wrong. Lots of scars heal. She inspected her legs again. They should have shown a zillion tiny scars from when Daddy tried teaching her to ride a bicycle. "Let go, Daddy. I can do it myself," she used to tell him all the time. Every time he believed her and released the bike, she toppled onto the ground.

One of the times she fell, the bicycle chain sliced her leg open. It took fourteen stitches to close the gap. Now she had to squint to see the fine white line reaching from her knee to her calf. Maybe that's the way the scars on her face would heal. After a long, long time. After the war was over and everyone was home safe again. And *ugly* would be just a word again.

She could do this. She could go to the movies. And she could look in the mirror, too. Eleanor wiped her palms on her skirt and then placed them on the glass. She lifted first one finger and then another and another. Quickly, she dropped them again, pushing hard against the mirror, smothering her reflection. "Honey, some things take a little while," Daddy had said after picking her up for about the hundredth time.

The whole time Eleanor was walking to the Rialto, her fingers picked at the smocking along the neck. Mama's dress was pretty, but it scratched the skin on her collarbone. At the intersection of Fowler Street and Belmont Avenue, she stopped and looked up at the theater's marquee. *Days of Glory,* it read. Her foot poised on the curbing. *Just like riding a bicycle, Eleanor. You just have to practice.*

Clarice had already spotted her. From the sidewalk in front of the theater, she called out to Eleanor. "Hey, Eleanor! Right over here. We're over here."

The minute Eleanor crossed the street, Clarice hurried over to her. "You're hair looks really nice. And I love your dress. That blue is such a pretty color for you."

Like a spoiled ten-year-old, Susan drummed her fingers against her legs. "We've been waiting for more than ten minutes. Tony's probably left already. We said we would meet him at seven. Seven!" Susan's face wore a funny expression — half smirk, half frown. Susan wasn't just jealous. She was plain old-fashioned rude. With a capital *R.* At the Academy, Eleanor had always made friends with the new girls. *I'm nicer than Susan. I never wanted anyone to feel uncomfortable.*

"Then we should be just fine," Eleanor said. "The clock at the bank hasn't even chimed the hour yet."

Tony walked up to the Rialto's ticket booth, his hands shoved in his pockets. He had that awkward, nervous look, like the scarecrow in *Wizard of Oz.* He didn't wave when he saw the girls, but he straightened up and let his arms fall to his sides. His gaze rested briefly on Eleanor. "Everybody looks real nice," he said. His voice cracked. "Are you ready to go inside?"

But *inside* meant the lobby. Even before Tony guided them through the open doors, Eleanor's knees began to wobble. She took huge gulps of air. *Count to ten. Slowly, Eleanor. Practice being brave. You can be brave just this once.*

"No, I don't want any popcorn," she snapped in response to Tony's hesitant question, then stood against one wall while Clarice and Susan waited with him in the snack line. Couples walked past her, holding hands as if they had been soldered together. Some of them snuck quick glances at Eleanor. She looked away. She checked for exit signs. She counted how many people stood outside the theater, waiting for tickets. The only thing that kept her from running out of the Rialto was the smell of popcorn and cotton candy. It reminded her of Friday nights in a whole other time, in a whole other world, and she clung to those memories until Clarice touched her elbow. "We're all set," she said.

Inside the theater, Eleanor found a seat near the back, as far from the center aisle as possible. Clarice sat beside her. Susan pushed Tony into a seat two rows ahead.

The second the lights dimmed, Eleanor's whole body relaxed. In the dark theater, she could laugh with Clarice and not worry that her laughter might attract attention.

But it did. A group of boys found seats behind the girls, and one of them kept kicking her chair with his foot.

"Your mother let you out this late on a Saturday night?" she asked, keeping her face averted.

"You don't know nothing," one boy said. His voice squeaked on "nothing," and he cleared his throat as Eleanor and Clarice giggled.

"They snuck out of the house to be with the grown-ups tonight," Clarice whispered. Then she spoke a little louder. "Isn't this way past your bedtime, little boys?"

The boys whispered and chattered behind them, and the bravest answered, "You think you know so much? We're going in the army tomorrow. It's our last night of freedom before we get shipped overseas."

"You're joining *which* army? The Defense League for Cub Scouts?" It came back to Eleanor in a flash — the flirting, the rhythm of the words. She had always been good at it. Marybeth — the thought hurt — Marybeth had always let her do the talking. "You're smarter than me," Marybeth said too many times. "It takes me all day to think up an answer, but not you. You're really smart that way."

Clarice nudged her elbow. "This is fun," she mouthed, but her words were a question.

The boys behind her whispered some more. "Shh. I'm trying to watch this," she said, trying to sound like Sister Agnes settling a class of freshman girls.

"Ah, we seen better movies this afternoon," one boy announced. The others shushed him. Eleanor wanted to laugh. Clarice was already laughing, her shoulders bouncing up and down. Susan and Tony? Eleanor could see the top of their heads. Tony's dark head never moved. He sat as rigidly as a statue. He hadn't taken Susan's hand. Eleanor could tell by the way Susan slumped in her seat. If Susan had been nicer, Eleanor could have told her how to get Tony to take her hand. Susan tried too hard; she looked too admiringly at him. *Pathetic,* Eleanor thought and then banished the word. She didn't like that word anymore.

She settled against the back of the seat. How beautiful Gregory Peck was. She had never thought of men as beautiful before. Was Robert beautiful like Gregory Peck? Her fingers touched her cheek, a feather-like touch. Not that it mattered. How could it possibly matter? Especially to her.

Gregory Peck dealt with Russians and the Eastern Front and all that "love stuff" Lindy complained about. Eleanor was still sniffling when the movie ended and the credits appeared on the screen. How could a person say good-bye to someone he loved so much? Clarice must have felt the same way. When the lights came up, she was wiping her eyes with her handkerchief.

The boy sitting behind Eleanor gave one last kick at her chair and began singing, "Goodnight, ladies, goodnight . . ." One of his friends' interrupted. "We got to get out of here, Tommy. My mom will kill me if I get home after nine-thirty." Their feet pounded up the aisle.

Eleanor didn't move.

"Lots of people here tonight," Clarice said. "I like to wait until everyone leaves, don't you? My eyes adjust to the light that way. Otherwise, I walk into the lobby and I'm blind as a bat. You know what I mean?"

They sat until the last person trudged up the aisle and the lights flickered once. "Thank you," Eleanor whispered.

Clarice didn't answer. She stood and stretched. "The best movies are the ones that make you cry a little. Don't you think so?" she asked as they headed toward the back.

Susan was standing beside Tony by the exit, tapping her foot on the carpet.

"You took long enough," she scolded as Clarice and

Eleanor approached. "The second show's gonna start any minute, and I'm not sitting through it again. It wasn't that good the first time."

What Susan really didn't like, Eleanor guessed, was Tony's shyness. He didn't take Susan's hand as they walked through the empty lobby. He didn't rest his palm on her back when they pushed through the doors to the outside.

"I'm hungry," Susan announced. "I want something to eat."

Clarice agreed. "I could go for about ten cups of slush. I'm so hot my fingertips are sweating."

"You had slush before?"

It took a moment for Eleanor to realize Tony was speaking to her. Once, when Jack Carmody had taken her to a restaurant near Beachmont Park, he had bought them each a cup of lemon slush on the way home. The ice had frozen her mouth, giving her an immediate headache, and Jack had laughed and tried to kiss the pain away. But she wouldn't let him.

"I've had it before," she said. But slush meant Beachmont Park and all those couples holding hands and mooning over each other, bringing back too many memories of another summer night in a whole other lifetime. "Can we go inside someplace instead?"

Tony tucked his hands into his pockets. "There's a Tubby's Custard by the railroad station. It's pretty quiet there this time of night."

Susan shook her head. "I want to go to the Belmont Diner. It's just a couple of blocks from here."

Susan pushed her way through the diner's front door. Eleanor followed her. The old couple in the front booth stared as she walked by, but Eleanor kept her eyes on Susan. "Can we sit closer to the door?" she asked. Susan ignored her. When they reached the very last booth, Susan slid into the farthest seat. Eleanor took the seat opposite her. She wasn't about to place her body within touching distance of such a rude person. And she had to bite her cheek to keep from smiling when Tony dropped into the seat next to her. It served Susan right.

At first, only Clarice talked. Only Clarice looked the waitress in the face and smiled brightly. "I'm having a strong lemonade," she said, winking at Susan as if this were some joke just between the two of them.

"French fries," Susan said. "And lemonade, too."

"Just lemonade for me," Eleanor said. Watching the movie had been fun. Teasing those younger boys had been fun. Sitting across from unsmiling Susan didn't feel like fun. Her neck had started itching again. She had the hardest time keeping her hands on the table.

"And I'll have a lemonade and an order of fries," Tony said.

The waitress left without comment.

A whole group of high school–aged boys and girls pushed their way through the diner's doors and settled by the front.

"Do we know them?" Clarice whispered to Susan.

Susan inspected the group. "Nope," she said.

The group was loud, and every second of their conversation was punctuated with laughter. Eleanor kept her eyes on the table while Clarice and Susan and even Tony talked around her. Their conversation sounded like some radio show she could barely hear through the static from a thunderstorm.

Then the laughter turned on her. Clarice and Tony were too busy talking to notice. They were discussing which English teacher Clarice and Susan were likely to get come September, and Tony, not shy or awkward for once, gave his opinion of each possibility. But Eleanor could feel the difference in the other group's conversation. She didn't have to see their faces to know that the sudden quiet, the whispering, the deep chuckles, and then the crescendo of voices were all about her. She peeked once. A smaller boy was staring right at her, his face contorted by a grin. He looked away quickly. He whispered something to the girl sitting next to him, and the girl's laughter peeled through the diner.

Susan's head bobbed back and forth, stealing looks at the laughing boy and then at Clarice and Tony. A tiny smile curled her lips, and her fingers tapped against the table.

"I have to leave," Eleanor announced. She shoved Tony with both hands. "Please let me out."

"What?" Tony didn't move.

"I have to leave. Now." She shoved again, as hard as she could, until he stood.

"Toasted," the smaller boy was saying. Eleanor could hear the words as if he had shouted them in her ear. "Toasted like a marshmallow."

Eleanor didn't wait for anyone to follow her. She pushed past Tony and hurried up the aisle. Out the door she flew, past the group that was laughing, past the surprised waitress, past the old couple in the front booth. She couldn't feel the tips of her fingers. She couldn't feel her feet. "Toasted." The word made her sick to her stomach.

Clarice caught up with Eleanor outside. "Eleanor, what is it? Are you all right?"

The collar of Eleanor's dress scraped against her scars and she tore at the smocking with trembling hands, ripping at the stitches until the material hung in tatters around her neck. Then she noticed Tony and Susan standing behind Clarice. She stiffened. *Mustn't let them see me cry. Mustn't let Susan know how hurt I am.* Never, never could she let *anyone* know how hurt she was. She forced her hands away from her collar and stared at a passing streetcar. But her anger curled inside her chest like a wild animal poised to attack.

Susan started to complain. "We never even had a chance to eat — "

The creature inside Eleanor exploded. "Are you happy? You got what you wanted, didn't you. All those other kids in there. Was it fun for you, Susan, knowing they were laughing at me? Are you truly happy now?"

But Susan wasn't smiling. "I didn't know," she kept repeating. "I'm sorry. I didn't think. I didn't know."

" 'I didn't think. I didn't know.' You want to know what it feels like to be me — people laughing, people staring? It feels like death, Susan. It feels as if I have nothing left inside — all the time." The creature released Eleanor's body with a whoosh. "So now you know," she said. "Now you all know."

Clarice refused to let Eleanor walk home alone. "We're

going with you," she insisted. "It's late and it's dark, and I don't want to worry about you."

They accompanied her to the end of Everett Street. "That's far enough," Eleanor announced. "I live right down the street from here."

"It's a nice street, Eleanor. Right near the ocean and everything." Tony said. He stood with his hands clenched at his sides. He and Clarice belonged together. They had the same kind eyes. They would have kind children who would never on earth make fun of anyone for the way that person looked.

Clarice squeezed Eleanor's hand. "You'll be all right?"

"I'm fine."

"I'm sorry," Susan said for the hundredth time. Eleanor heard the apology through a haze of pain that swirled around her, sucking her up in its whirlwind.

"I'm fine," Eleanor said again. She waited until Clarice and Tony and Susan turned the corner onto Whittin Avenue. Then she turned left toward Mahoney's Point, toward the ocean.

She climbed onto the sea wall and sat. No moon lit the ocean tonight, and she missed its comforting shine. But she could smell the saltwater and hear the rush of waves against the shore. The ocean was the only safe haven from those Susan storms and Robert storms and all the terrible storms in her life. Home meant seeing Mama and having to explain what had happened to the dress. Home meant Lindy waiting up to hear every detail of the night — Lindy, who thought her big sister was a far better person than Eleanor could ever be.

People sometimes slipped into the ocean and were never heard from again. She had thought about that before — about slipping into the sea and losing herself in the waves. When she first came home from the hospital, when Gram's eyes filled with tears the first time she saw Eleanor's face, when Mama told Eleanor and Lindy that they would have to move from their house on Cape Ann. Each time, Eleanor wanted to find the ocean and become part of it.

But that would mean the fire had won.

Beautiful night. The stars glittered like diamonds strewn across a black velvet sky. Eleanor loved night. She loved it almost as much as she loved the ocean. Night made her the same as everyone else.

If she could, she would wrap the whole beautiful sky around her, and no one would ever see her scars again. Instead of becoming part of the ocean, she could become part of the night.

Chapter Nine

❧ ❧

"Hello, Eleanor? This is Clarice Michaud. From the drugstore?"

It was the third time Clarice had telephoned this morning. The first time, she wanted to know if Eleanor thought Gregory Peck was as handsome as people said. The second time, she asked if Eleanor were going to work on Tuesday, as if Eleanor hadn't worked every Tuesday since she started at the drugstore. Each time she called, her voice sounded a little hesitant. Each time, Eleanor's hand gripped the receiver so tightly that the muscles in her fingers cramped in protest.

"I was just wondering — Tony was wondering, too — about driving? He's going to teach Susan and me, and he wanted to know — and I do, too — if you want to learn with us."

Eleanor held the receiver away from her ear. Clarice's voice still came through. "I mean, it wouldn't be today or tomorrow. But next Saturday, maybe."

The world could disappear by next Saturday! New York could be bombed. The German army could land in little old Beachmont, Massachusetts. How could Eleanor possibly plan that far in advance?

"He asked — Tony did — right after church. When we were standing on the steps outside. He asked if you wanted to learn how to drive."

"Clarice, I'm fine. That's what you really want to know. Tell Tony I'm fine. Tell Susan she doesn't have to feel guilty anymore. I'm fine."

Eleanor didn't slam down the receiver, but she didn't say good-bye, either. When she looked up, Mama was standing in the doorway to the living room. She held the blue dress in her hand.

"I found this at the bottom of your closet. What happened to the neck, Eleanor?"

"I always give you the clothes I need washed. You don't have to go sneaking into my things that way. It's my business."

Mama folded the dress, first the sleeves and then the skirt, until the neck of the dress was hidden in the folds. "Eleanor, when you came home last night, you never said a word except 'I'm going to bed now.' You snapped at Lindy at breakfast when she asked how the movie was. Sweetie . . ." She rubbed her eyes with her free hand. "How can I help you if you don't tell me what's bothering you?"

The angry creature inside Eleanor stirred. She took deep breaths. The whole time Eleanor was in the hospital, Mama had changed her sheets and her bedpan. Mama had cut Eleanor's food into bite-sized pieces. Mama had helped so much, but now Eleanor was tired of that help. "You need to leave me alone, Mama. I'll be fine if you just leave me alone."

Mama turned and walked out of the room.

Right before lunchtime, Mama tried again. She sat on the bed next to Eleanor and coaxed. "Sweetie, please tell me."

Eleanor whispered. "I told you. I'll be fine."

Mama's lips brushed Eleanor's cheek. "You know I'm always here if you need me," she said.

"Please! If you could just let me be unhappy for a while. That's all. I just need to be sad a little while."

Mama sighed and pushed herself off the bed. "When you're ready, there's a chicken salad sandwich in the icebox." She dug into her apron pocket and dropped an envelope onto the bureau. "You have a letter, too."

The whole world exploded into fireworks like the biggest Fourth of July display on earth. *Robert!* Immediately, the logical part of Eleanor's brain doused the celebration. *Not possible. Not so soon after the other one.* But she had the hardest time not hurrying right over and grabbing the envelope. Mama was standing by the door. One hand rested on her hip. She fanned her face with the other.

"It's too hot to do much," she said. "But I told Lindy I'd teach her how to play cards. Why don't you play, too? When you're finished reading your letter."

"I might. Later maybe. Thank you, Mama. For bringing my letter." But Mama was already gone.

Eleanor waited two complete heartbeats before she leaped off the bed. She stubbed her toe on the post, but she didn't stop to rub the pain away. What was red and blue and white all over? An envelope. Like the one sitting on the bureau. The one addressed to her in that familiar bold handwriting. She ripped open the flap and pulled out the letter. The paper was creamy white this time, and Robert had used a pen.

July 3, 1944

Dear Eleanor,

I must have sounded heartless in my last letter. I didn't mean to.

You wouldn't be you if you didn't care about people so much. You should be a writer, Eleanor. You make people feel things with your words.

I did *mean it when I said I hope nothing bad ever happens to you.*

Take care of yourself.

Affectionately yours,
Robert

Eleanor pressed the letter to her lips and kissed his name.

She searched in the top drawer for Daddy's fountain pen. *It's here. It's got to be here somewhere.* But all she found were four pencils with half-eaten erasers and one of Cinderella's tiny black velvet shoes. *Lindy!* She'd gotten into Eleanor's things again.

She checked in Lindy's drawers, pushing aside panties and undershirts and socks. No pen. She rummaged through the books and doll clothes and drawings under Lindy's bed. Still no pen. She found it at last under Lindy's pillow, along with a sheet of paper blank except for the heading, *Deer Robrt.*

I'll have to tell Robert that, she thought.

But Eleanor had the hardest time telling Robert anything. She started the letter.

Dear Robert,

It's Saturday, and I'm sitting here on a hotter than the hinges of you-know-where afternoon.

She stopped writing. She crossed out every word. Her toes wouldn't stay still. They wiggled so much that she had to kick off her socks to give them more room. Her shoulders kept bouncing up and down like the ball she and Lindy had used to play Colors with. That made her back twitch.

Her mind was all a tizzy. That's what Marybeth used to say whenever she was excited about something.

She should call Marybeth and tell her about Robert.

She should call Clarice and *not* tell her about Robert. Just apologize for being such a baby last night. Because there was no reason on earth to be so sensitive, not in a world where boys like Robert wrote wonderful letters to girls like her.

Lindy was spilling cards all over the kitchen table when Eleanor entered.

"Mama's teaching me to shuffle the deck," Lindy said.

"And you're doing very well," Mama said. She winked at Eleanor. "Almost as well as I'm doing at cooking."

Eleanor dropped into the chair next to Mama. "Since we're talking about learning things, how would it be if I learned how to drive?"

Lindy abandoned the cards. "Drive a car? Like Mrs. Carvelli? Can we go for a ride tomorrow?"

"I won't be able to drive by tomorrow, Lindy. I have to

learn how. Like you learned to swim, remember? It takes practice."

"Driving isn't that easy, Eleanor," Mama said. "Daddy tried to teach me, but well . . ." She tried to smile. "I wasn't a very good student."

Lindy bounced out of the chair. "You could drive us to Cape Ann, and I could see Peggy again. She's my best friend except for Jeannie, and she hasn't even met Cinderella."

Mama's face wore that pinched look. "I don't know about that, Lindy. Don't forget, we're trying to save gas for the soldiers. To help them win the war." Then she turned to Eleanor. "I'm just not sure about this, Eleanor. You would have to have a very good teacher — somebody experienced and responsible."

"Clarice and Susan's friend Tony has taught lots of people. That's what Clarice said."

The cards lay on the table — some face up, some face down. Mama picked them up one by one and arranged them into piles according to suit. "I suppose it's all right if you're very careful. Daddy always wanted you to learn."

"Thank you," Eleanor said. She rested her cheek against Mama's shoulder. "For so much, Mama."

Clarice answered the phone on the very first ring. "Hello?"

Eleanor didn't say hello back. "About driving next Saturday? I'd like to go, if that's still okay with you. I really do want to learn."

"I'm so glad, Eleanor. We'll have so much fun." There was silence on the line for endless seconds. "I think Susan was mean last night. That's what I've been wanting to say to you.

She doesn't think. It's not personal. But I wanted you to know how I felt."

"It really is okay, Clarice. People don't understand. They do things or say things they don't mean." *Or write things.*

"I — well — I really do think you're very brave. It must have been awful for you. The fire, I mean."

When Eleanor was in the hospital, and for months after she got out, Marybeth and she had talked about life before the fire and life after the fire, but they had never really talked about what happened that night. "It *was* awful, Clarice." Eleanor said gently. "I'll see you Tuesday at work."

It was evening before Eleanor stopped feeling as if the top of her head would explode from too much happiness. "I'm going to Mahoney's Point for a while," Eleanor told Mama. Mama sat on the front porch swing with Mrs. Carvelli. A book lay unopened on her lap. Mrs. Carvelli didn't keep quiet long enough for anyone nearby to read.

"Don't be too late."

Mrs. Carvelli had to add her two cents' worth. "You just be careful when you're walking home. You never know. My cousin says they spotted a German sub right out in Boston Harbor. Never know when they'll be sneaking around, grabbing young girls — "

"Shh!" Mama hissed, pointing to Lindy and Jeannie playing Witch Are You Coming on the stairs. The *shh* quieted Mrs. Carvelli for a whole twenty seconds.

Next door, Mrs. Beauchamp practiced the scales on the piano in her living room. The Derrivans down the street had their windows open wide, and Eleanor could hear Carl Simons from WBZ announcing which song would be played next. Across the street, Mr. and Mrs. Sullivan pushed back and forth on their rocking chairs. Every once in a while, Mrs. Sullivan yelled out to one of the grandchildren kicking a soccer ball in the street, "Children who play in traffic don't generally become adults." The grandchildren argued and laughed and kicked the soccer ball so hard Eleanor could hear the *thwomp* as their feet connected with the leather.

Eleanor sat on the bottom stair and let her chin rest against the back of her hand. How magical everyday sounds were. They gave her a safe, warm place where she could lose herself in memories.

It had been like that in Cape Ann, too. Mama had always hummed while she "put on her face" to go out dancing with Daddy. And he whistled while he shaved — a shrill whistle that hurt Eleanor's ears. He laughed when Eleanor covered them. He laughed even harder when she tried whistling herself. She pursed her lips and blew as hard as she could, but no sound came out. "You have to curl your tongue," Daddy said and demonstrated for her.

But no matter how many times Daddy showed her, Eleanor couldn't curl her tongue correctly. And now, the sound of whistling hurt her heart more than her ears.

Eleanor still had a letter to write. She pushed her hand inside her skirt pocket. The stationery and the pen were safely tucked inside.

"You must have a boyfriend down by the beach or

something," Mrs. Carvelli said. "Seems like you go there a thousand times a day."

Lindy spoke right up. "Ellie's boyfriend doesn't live near here."

Eleanor's eyes drilled right into Lindy's.

Lindy took a step backward. "What? What's the matter?"

"My boyfriend doesn't live here because I don't have one." Just wait until she got Little Miss Bigmouth alone.

Mrs. Carvelli's tiny eyes grew even tinier. "No skin off my nose if you want to keep your private life private. I mind my own business. Like I says to Chubbs, what a young girl does is her business. And her Mama's."

"I'm so glad," Eleanor said. "My father always told me, 'Mind your own business is the eleventh commandment.'"

She felt Mama's hand on her arm. "Get some ice cream on the way home, sweetie. We all need to cool off a little. There's money in the teapot."

Eleanor shook off Mama's hand. "I don't need money, Mama. I've got some of my own."

"Chocolate. Cinderella wants chocolate. With sprinkles," Lindy announced. Her voice almost drowned out the sound of Mama's sigh.

"What does Jeannie want?" Eleanor asked. She had avoided looking at the little girl, but now Jeannie tugged at Eleanor's blouse, pulling Eleanor's face down near her own.

"I like strawberry," she whispered. "But I don't like sprinkles very much." Her lips almost touched Eleanor's scarred cheek.

Eleanor closed her eyelids for just a moment. When she

opened them, no one was looking at her. Mama's attention was suddenly taken by the book in her lap, Mrs. Carvelli glared at the Sullivan twins, who took turns kicking the now-deflated ball across the road. "Hey, you guys!" she yelled. "You wanna get killed or something?" Lindy and Jeannie admired Mrs. Carvelli's newest creation for Cinderella, lifting up the blue satin skirt and inspecting the stitches on the hem.

"I have to go," Eleanor said to no one in particular.

July 8, 1944

Dear Robert,

First of all, happy Fourth of July a whole four days late. After nights of cherry bomb explosions and firecrackers, the Beachmont natives are finally resting.

Most days and nights, the city reminds me of Mrs. Carvelli — noisy and rude. But then there are some evenings when Beachmont is more like a town, more like the place where I grew up, where you sat on your porch and listened to neighbors calling to each other.

You can tell by my description that not much is happening around here. Mrs. Williams hasn't been herself lately. She's worried about her son, and I can't blame her for being a wreck. He's in the middle of all that fighting going on in the Pacific.

I went to the movies last night with some friends. I haven't been in a movie theater for the longest time. I can remember the very first movie I ever saw. It was a Shirley Temple one. She was singing and dancing and her curls bobbed up and down. I wanted to be just like her. In our backyard, I would put on a show for an imaginary audience, tap dancing on the grass even though I had no idea how to dance. It must have been quite a spectacle to watch.

Soon, Mama will be enrolling Lindy and me in school. One more year and I'll be finished with grades and homework and classes that are so boring I could scream. I haven't decided about college. Maybe you're right about me becoming a writer. I do like to put words down on paper. It makes me feel as if I can capture things forever.

I'm at sitting at Mahoney's Point right now. Sometimes when I look out at the ocean, I feel the waves as if they are right inside me. When I was little and Mama would take us to the beach, I'd spend all day in the water, until my hands and toes were wrinkled like prunes and my hair was stiff with salt. Daddy used to call me his little water baby. And when it came time to leave, I always started to cry.

Mama always asked what the matter was.

But I couldn't explain.

At night, I'd lie on top of the sheets and still feel the waves lapping against my stomach. I loved that feeling. I haven't felt it in a long time. I haven't been in the water in a long time.

She almost added "not since I was burned." Her pen poised over the paper. *Tell him, Eleanor. He will understand. He won't hate you.*

But her fingers cramped suddenly, and she could barely scrawl an ending.

Please stay safe, Robert.

> *Affectionately yours,*
> *Eleanor*

Chapter Ten

❧ ❧

July 12, 1944

*D*ear Robert,

I don't know how to break this to you. Especially after all I said about Mrs. Carvelli being a secret weapon if she ever learned to drive. The horrible truth is, I am a worse driver than she could ever dream of being.

This morning was my first driving lesson. Clarice and Susan talked Mr. Carvelli into loaning us his Buick so a friend of theirs, Tony, could teach us how to drive.

So we all piled into the car, and Tony drove us to the back side of Ocean Avenue. "You can't hit much more than sand and a few beach roses that way," he said. "So who wants to drive first?"

Clarice and Susan kept arguing about how wide the window should be open and whether frizzy hair looked worse than straight hair after the wind gets to it. "I'll be your first victim," I volunteered and climbed into the driver's seat.

As Lindy says, cross my heart and hope to die, I followed

Tony's directions exactly. "Push your left foot down on the clutch," he said. "Give the car a little gas with your right foot." But instead of moving forward, the Buick started lurching like a sick cow.

"You've got to let up on the clutch a little," Tony said.

I tried. The lurching stopped all right. All of a sudden, we heard this terrible screeching, and Tony began shouting at me, "You're stripping the gears! Throw out the clutch. Throw out the clutch!"

So I threw it out. Let me tell you. At least when the car was dying, it stayed on the roadway. Whatever I did this time sent the Buick halfway across the street into some bushes. Actually, the hood did look kind of pretty with all those roses decorating it.

Tony didn't think so. You would have thought the car belonged to him, the way he acted. First he asked if everyone was all right, then he turned to me, his eyes blazing.

I tried to explain. "You told me to throw out the clutch."

"You're supposed to push down. Release it."

"Well, why didn't you say that? I thought you wanted me to let go. Throw it out. You know. Like garbage. You let it go!"

He sighed. "It's not the same with cars."

The way Tony's worry lines showed white against his forehead, I know exactly what he will look like when he is an old man. And Clarice's and Susan's mouths were open and moving, but no words escaped. They weren't worrying about hair right then. But everyone looked so ridiculous, I couldn't help laughing. Pretty soon, Clarice and Susan started. Even Tony joined in. We laughed so loudly we must have scared

*every gull for miles. Actually, I'm surprised you didn't hear us
all the way to New York City.*

   *"That's enough driving for one day," Tony finally managed
to say.*

   "What about us?" Susan complained.

   He gave her such a look.

   *I can't blame him. Now he'll be too chicken to take anyone
driving ever again, and it's all my fault.*

   *I'm sorry about the long letter, but I just had to tell
someone. My mother would die if she ever knew.*

   Please stay safe, Robert. I'll try to stay safe, too.

Affectionately yours,
Secret Weapon Eleanor

Eleanor loved writing the letter. She loved picking and
choosing exactly the details she wanted Robert to know. She
didn't have to tell him how Susan pouted the whole way
home, or how Clarice filled the silence by chattering away
like a little bird. She didn't have to mention that sitting next
to Tony made her more nervous than the actual driving, and
how she felt as if her scars were on display for the whole
world to see. Instead, Eleanor could lose herself in the words
and become the girl Robert imagined her to be. Writing was
just like acting, except you didn't have to show your face to
anyone.

"What are you doing?" Lindy wanted to know. She flopped
onto the bed and leaned her head on Eleanor's shoulder. "Are
you writing to Robert again?"

"That's what friends do," Eleanor said. The warmth of Lindy's body against hers filled Eleanor with tenderness. Lindy was so much like Daddy, interested in everything and everyone on earth. Eleanor used to cringe when she and Daddy waited for a streetcar, and he began talking to people waiting at the same stop. It didn't matter if their clothes were ragged or their hands were filthy. Daddy treated everyone with the same respect he gave to his most important patients.

Lindy treated people the same way.

Eleanor wrapped her arm around her sister's shoulders and squeezed until Lindy squeaked in protest. "Read me the letter," Lindy demanded. She propped herself on her elbows, her head cocked. "I love Robert," she said. "He knows my name and everything."

How simple life was for Lindy. She could blurt out whatever was in her head without being afraid of what people might think.

"Dear Robert . . ." Eleanor began reading. She couldn't help laughing out loud as she read her description of poor Tony's shattered nerves. But Lindy didn't understand her humor the way Robert would. "Does that mean you can get your license now?" she asked when Eleanor finished.

"It means I'll be lucky if Tony ever gets in the car with me again."

"Mrs. Carvelli was practicing with another lady yesterday. She was driving just like a real person, right down the road and everything."

Eleanor tweaked Lindy's ear. "Mrs. Carvelli could walk on water, too, I bet."

At supper, Mama said the same thing in a slightly different way when Lindy showed them a pink gown Mrs. Carvelli had made for Cinderella.

"Look at this embroidery, Eleanor. It's exquisite." Mama straightened her shoulders. "I'm going right downstairs and thank her. Then I'm going to invite her up for a cup of coffee. It's high time. The woman has been more than generous to us."

The funny thing was, Mrs. Carvelli acted almost humble when she sat down with them in the kitchen. "You got a nice table here," she said, running her hands along the top. "With a drawer in the middle, just like you see in those fancy magazines. My table, it's the one Papa gave us for a wedding present. Long time ago now."

"The sewing on Cinderella's dress is beautiful, Mrs. Carvelli," Mama said.

Lindy sat next to Mrs. Carvelli. "And it's pink, too. Pink's my favorite color. Mrs. Carvelli says I'm pretty in pink." She leaned her head against Mrs. Carvelli's arm.

"*Very* pretty. But hey, all of you should be calling me Angela by now," Mrs. Carvelli said. "No standing on ceremony with neighbors, right? Besides, sewing's like nothing at all. I love sewing. Me and Chubbs, if we had any kids, I would've sewed all their clothes — the boys', too. Mrs. Adams was my sewing teacher. She said I had the best stitching she ever saw at Washington Heights."

Mama's expression reminded Eleanor of the time Lindy came home, bragging about all the A's on her report card. "You would have made a wonderful mother, Angela," Mama said.

"Oh, sure I would have. Ten kids, that's what Chubbs and me always talked about. But you know how things are. They don't work out the way you think. First one baby, then another and another. Six times we tried. And six times, they died before being born. That's when I said enough. I wasn't breaking my heart again."

Mama reached her hand across the table and patted Mrs. Carvelli's arm.

Mrs. Carvelli brushed Mama's hand away. "*Sheesh.* You'd think we got nothing better to talk about than yesterday's news." Now her voice had that raspy "yelling-across-the-street" sound to it. "My papa always told me that things happen for a reason. Things like you losing your husband and Eleanor losing her looks."

Mama's eyes were about to fall out of her head, but she said nothing. The silence was so thick that Eleanor had trouble breathing. She couldn't bear it a moment longer. "Would you like another cup of coffee, Angela?" she asked.

Mrs. Carvelli wiped her eyes with the back of her hand. "You got none of the good stuff left, huh? They mix one crummy coffee bean in a pound of chicory and pretend that's coffee. I swear, the ration board is just trying to see how miserable they can make us." She wiped her eyes again. "I'm telling you, it's hot enough to fry eggs without a stove. That's what they'll be rationing next — stoves and iceboxes." Mrs. Carvelli sounded just the way Eleanor did sometimes, when she didn't want anyone to know how much she hurt. Daddy would have understood, though. He always said the best way to find out what was wrong with people was to look into their eyes. "You can't hide what's inside," he explained. Now, when Eleanor looked into Mrs. Carvelli's eyes, she saw sadness and a touch of anger. And bewilderment as well.

Eleanor thought about Mrs. Carvelli as she sat at her bedroom window and looked at the sidewalk below. Lindy was playing jacks with Jeannie. The two little girls giggled and fought and made up and fought again.

"Jeannie says her uncle's not coming home after the war," Lindy had reported just this morning. She didn't ask what that meant, which was just as well because Eleanor wouldn't know how to explain.

She reached up and touched her cheek. For those few moments this afternoon, after she'd crashed the car, she forgot her face. She forgot everything except the pain in her stomach from laughing. If only home could be like that. The small rooms and musty smell weren't what made this apartment uncomfortable. What was missing was laughter. No wonder Lindy went searching for Mrs. Carvelli. Mama and Eleanor didn't laugh enough.

They used to. Before the fire, Mama would fix Sunday dinner after church, and Daddy would settle at the kitchen table with the Sunday paper. He didn't read much of it. Mostly, he and Mama talked — about old Gertie Ferguson and her snoring during the sermon, or how the Watsons were going to have their hands full with those twin boys after dealing with four well-behaved girls. Daddy and everyone laughed. That was the best part of being together — the laughter.

At least she could make Robert laugh with her letters. She folded the pages carefully into an envelope. When she placed it on the front hall table, she was surprised to find a red-and-blue-bordered letter waiting there for her.

July 10, 1944

Dear Eleanor,

I'm envious of you, going to the movies like that. I'm even more envious of people who knew you as that little girl who pretended to be Shirley Temple.

Supposedly, we are moving out today, tomorrow, next week, next month. No one really knows. Leave it to the army. They keep us hanging on month after month, and suddenly we're on the next boat to help the war effort.

This isn't the easiest thing to admit, but I'm feeling nervous about the whole thing. I don't think I could tell anyone else that, Eleanor.

In my thoughts, I tell you a lot of things. It's as if we are sitting across the table from each other, discussing the day's events. We know so much about each other. You can probably name my favorite color and my favorite food. And I see your family and the Carvellis and Mrs. Williams as if they are standing in front of me.

But I never see you. I try to picture you sometimes. You have dark hair, or maybe it's light. Are you tall or short? Do you have brown eyes or eyes as blue as the ocean you love so much? Not that it makes any difference how you look. It's just that I know everything about you except for this one thing.

You must wonder about me, too. That's why I'm sending you

a picture with this letter. One of my buddies took it last spring when we were standing in Times Square. I wonder if you could do the same in your next letter — send me a picture?

Please don't think I'm rude for asking. If you don't want to send it along, I will understand.

Take good care of yourself, Eleanor.

Affectionately yours,
Robert

Except for this one thing, Robert had written. Eleanor looked at his face, at the curve of his cheek — still more boy than man. He had a gentle mouth and truly beautiful eyes. And he would be going overseas soon, far from the safety of New York. She tried to concentrate on his fear first, imagining him hurt and calling for her, or perhaps blinded and coming home. She could read to him then, or sit with him on park benches and describe the birds and the trees and the children playing there. He would never have to know about her face.

If he didn't see her picture beforehand, that is. Her picture. Eleanor wished she could find a hole somewhere, so she could crawl inside and never come out. Never mind crawling inside the hole. She *was* the hole — a huge, gaping ache that kept getting deeper. Her arms reached around her shoulders, hugging them as she rocked back and forth.

She remembered Jack Carmody taking her to Littlefield's Restaurant one evening. They sat on the porch, drinking lemonade and watching boats slip in and out of their slip docks — sleek, long ones with sails like starched napkins;

shorter, chubbier ones that putt-putted through the harbor until they reached the open sea and suddenly became graceful.

Jack stared at one long-faced girl who had tiny eyes and black hair that slumped over her shoulders. She stood on the dock and giggled at the clumsiness of a boy on a boat nearby. "What a dog!" Jack said, too loudly. His voice dripped with contempt. "I can't imagine any guy wanting to be seen with a dog like her — never mind actually *touching* her." The girl turned as he spoke the words. She must have heard at least part of what he said, because her face collapsed as if she had been slapped. Eleanor thought her stomach had collapsed. *You're a mean person, Jack Carmody.*

She had stopped letting Jack steal kisses after that. Pretty soon, she stopped going places with him altogether. But she hadn't said a word to him that day. She never told him why she didn't want to see him anymore.

Eleanor couldn't let Robert see her face. Not now, not in this way. He didn't know her well enough. He didn't care enough about her yet. Eleanor knew exactly what would happen if she sent a picture. He would never ever see *her* again. He would see only her scars.

Her hands couldn't stop trembling. Her whole insides were trembling. She took the letter with her to the bathroom and stood in front of the mirror. She hadn't really inspected her face since that first time. And she had completely avoided seeing her body, pretending those scars didn't matter because they were hidden. For five minutes, she stood in front of the mirror with her hand on the top button of her blouse. But Eleanor couldn't pretend anymore.

Top button first, then the second and the third. With her eyes squeezed shut, she unbuttoned her blouse and removed it. So many times she had complained about her chest being too flat or her shoulders being too wide. Now she would give anything for small breasts and broad shoulders as long as they remained unmarked by the fire. But she knew they were not. Carefully, she opened one eye and then the other. She saw nothing for a moment.

All of a sudden, Eleanor felt so dizzy and sick she had to hold onto the wall to keep from fainting. But the feeling passed. She peered into the mirror. The person who looked back smiled unwillingly. The face didn't belong to a phantom anymore. But it didn't belong to Eleanor, either.

Toasted, just like a marshmallow, the boy in the diner had said. And he was right. The scars covered her face like someone had smeared the inside of a marshmallow all over her cheek and chin.

Poor Daddy. He had tried so hard. He had given Eleanor the smallpox vaccination on her left shoulder, so it wouldn't show when she was old enough to wear fancy dresses without sleeves. It was still there, white and puckery, half-hidden by her bra strap. And then there was her right side, covered with what looked like a million vaccination scars that had fused together over her shoulder and arm, spilling onto her chest and abdomen like sheets of white seersucker.

Those other doctors, they didn't fix you up so good, she whispered, in her best Mrs. Carvelli imitation.

If only she had met Robert before the fire. He would have loved her so much. He would have loved looking at her picture, taking it out of his wallet and showing it to his buddies. Because she had been pretty. Not beautiful, but she had had pretty skin and a dimple in her right cheek. And it was hard to remember, sometimes, that she wasn't *that* Eleanor anymore, that she didn't have a dimple in her cheek.

Send me a picture. Of course, Robert. She could send a picture, all right. She could send it, and then what? He would write. Of course he would write to her again. But he would write these really polite letters, and they would get shorter and shorter, and eventually they would stop coming. And she would never again feel what he was thinking, never know exactly how he reacted to something she wrote. He wouldn't tell her about his friends or his dog or if he were feeling afraid or guilty or show her all those secret places inside.

And that would absolutely break her heart. Because when Robert let her see those secret places, that's when she forgot most — forgot this toasted, ugly creature she had become.

Eleanor knew exactly what she should do. She should write a Dear John letter to Robert, telling him she had found someone else. Then it would be him who felt the hurt — his heart that would shatter every time the mail arrived with no letter from her.

But the words wouldn't come. She tried different openings.

Dear Robert, I am so sorry to tell you this . . .

Dear Robert, Just last week a really nice boy came into the drugstore.

Each time, she stopped. She imagined how she would feel

if she could never again look forward to the mail, could never open another envelope with red-and-blue borders.

In the back hall, under the carton of Haviland china, was a box filled with old pictures. Eleanor dug through the box. She pushed aside photographs of Daddy and Mama at the beach house, Lindy on her swing set, Eleanor in her cowgirl suit. The pictures belonged to another family. That family had parties and happy lives and Christmases with too many presents.

Finally, under all the other photographs, Eleanor found her school picture from sophomore year. She had never liked it very much. Her hair flopped over her shoulders instead of curling softly around them the way she had wanted. And she looked altogether too serious.

But her face was there, whole and unmarked.

She picked up the picture and held it so close to her face that her eyelashes touched the photograph, so close that she couldn't see the image anymore. She had to pull her face away so the tears dripping onto her cheeks wouldn't ruin it. Why did such a kind, pretty girl have to get so badly burned? It wasn't fair. Only bad people deserved to have bad things happen to them.

Eleanor shredded the letter she had written about the driving lesson and buried the pieces in the wastebasket. Now Lindy would never find them and ask questions that Eleanor didn't want to answer.

July 12, 1944

Dear Robert,

I don't blame you for being nervous about going overseas. I'd be petrified if I were you. But everyone says the war is going to end soon. Maybe it'll be over before you are transferred.

Thank you for your picture. You look younger than I imagined. But nice. Enclosed is a picture of me. I hope you like it.

Lindy has added your name to her prayers each night. If I didn't know better, I'd think it was the sweetest thing you ever saw, the way she gets down on her knees and goes through her list of people half a mile long. But I know better. Actually, she's plotting to stay up as late as possible. Oh, not in your case, of course. She adores it when you mention her in your letters. I think it makes her feel special.

Please stay safe, Robert.

Affectionately yours,
Eleanor

P.S. I had my first driving lesson today. How come, in the language of boys and men, "throw out the clutch" means to press down?

Chapter Eleven

❧ ❧

July 14, 1944

*D*ear Eleanor,

Your picture arrived in this morning's mail. Eleanor, it's funny how we have misconceptions about people. For example, you look more serious than I expected — and younger, too. In my imagination, you are always smiling. That may be because your letters make me smile. But you do have blue eyes. I knew that! My ocean girl just had to have blue eyes.

Eleanor blinked rapidly. "My ocean girl." Daddy's words. And that *My,* as in someone special just to him.

Congratulations on surviving your first driving lesson. I can understand why "throwing out the clutch" would be confusing. What's really happening is that you are releasing it every time you put your foot down. Don't get discouraged. Before my first driving lesson, I was convinced I knew everything there was to know about cars. My dad took me out to one of those back roads near our reservoir and handed me the keys. I drove into the nearest tree. Dad said, "I think we'll practice steering next."

I hope Mrs. Williams's son will be all right. I hope this war will be over soon, so everyone can go back home to be with family and friends.

Time flies. Tom O'Connor is waiting outside my door. He is undoubtedly practicing his French "mal lettres," as our instructor describes swearing. We were supposed to be hopping the subway half an hour ago to see a matinee in town. But I wanted to write to you first.

I enjoy your letters very much, Eleanor. Please take care of yourself. And please be careful the next time you "throw out the clutch."

Affectionately yours,
Robert

Mrs. Williams walked into the cubby just as Eleanor finished reading Robert's letter for the umpteenth time. Mrs. Williams didn't even say, "Good morning, Eleanor." She reached up to place her sweater and pocketbook on the coat rack.

"I'm sorry," she said when she bumped Eleanor's arm. She unfolded her apron and tied it around her waist.

Mrs. Williams's face was all blotchy and pink, and her eyes barely showed beneath swollen lids.

"Is there something wrong?" Eleanor asked.

Mrs. Williams looked past Eleanor toward the pharmacist's bench. "I have to talk to Chubbs," she said. "I have to tell him something."

In the back room, the two spoke in low voices. Eleanor couldn't hear their words, but she could understand their tones. Mr. Carvelli's was bewildered at first and then utterly sympathetic. Mrs. Williams sounded wretched. After the voices stopped, she came and stood in the doorway by Eleanor's cubby. Mr. Carvelli followed her, and if it hadn't been such a sad sight, it would have been funny — that little man placing his arm around that great big woman. But their faces broke Eleanor's heart.

"Is there something wrong?" Eleanor asked again.

Mrs. Williams looked like she had been shot. "It's my son," she said.

Of course. Eleanor should have recognized that anguished look right away. She had seen it on Daddy's face after he had lost a patient. She had seen it on Mama's face after Daddy died. *Dead. Michael's dead.*

"They came late last night and told me," Mrs. Williams said. "My beautiful boy . . ." Her voice trailed off. She sat down suddenly in the chair and covered her face with her hands. Eleanor knelt on the floor next to Mrs. Williams and patted her awkwardly on the back. "I'm sorry, Mrs. Williams. I'm so sorry."

Mrs. Williams had spoken of Michael so often that Eleanor could picture him — a tall, gangly twenty-year-old with hands the size of boulders. She could even imagine his voice, deep but with a telltale crack when he tried too hard to hide his emotions. "Oh, Ma, don't make such a big fuss," he would tell his mother when she introduced him as her son, the hero. "You're embarrassing me, Ma."

"I thought I should tell my friends in person," Mrs. Williams said. "And I had to do *something* besides think every minute, every second of the day. My brother and my sister Kate were there all night, trying to help. They talked about everything except Michael. They feel so bad for me, but they just don't understand." Her shrill voice hurt Eleanor's ears. "I want my son back!" she cried.

She lifted her head and spoke only to Eleanor. "I went into his room this morning. I picked up his sweatshirt. I could still smell his sweat, like he had just taken it off yesterday." Her voice softened to a whimper. "I used to yell at him about coming to the table all sweaty. But I wouldn't mind. Not now. If I could just hold him one more time."

Mrs. Williams started crying so hard Eleanor was afraid she would never be able to stop. Eleanor gulped and swallowed, but her own tears came anyway, soaking the collar of her blouse, dripping onto her hands. Customers may have come and gone, and perhaps Mr. Carvelli waited on them. Or perhaps he sent them away.

"I'm taking a little time off," Mrs. Williams said finally. "Chubbs told me I could. Just a while."

"Of course," Eleanor agreed.

"You'll be all right?" Mrs. Williams asked.

"We'll be fine here. You taught me everything I know."

"I don't mean the drugstore." She touched Eleanor's scarred cheek. "I mean you."

Her words made Eleanor's sight blur again. "You're going to make me drown in my own tears, Mrs. Williams. I'll be fine."

Mrs. Williams nodded. She stood without speaking and pulled her purse and sweater off the coat rack.

"If there is anything I can do, or anything you need . . ."

But Mrs. Williams wouldn't allow Eleanor to finish. "Nothing. There's nothing anyone can do right now," she said. "I'm going home. I don't know why. I can't think of anything else to do. You're a good girl, Eleanor. I know you'll take care of Chubbs and the store for me."

The telephone on the desk rang three times and then a fourth. "I have to answer that, Mrs. Williams. Mr. Carvelli must be busy with a customer." Eleanor lifted the receiver.

"Carvelli's Drugstore. May I help you?" The voice on the other end chattered on and on until Eleanor wanted to throw the telephone against the nearest wall. "Yes, of course we have Coke syrup. You can pick up a bottle any time. It should relieve your son's tummy upset. Yes, we still deliver." As if a stomachache really mattered in life. She wrote the customer's name on a blank pad, scribbling as fast as she could so she could get back to Mrs. Williams. But by the time she finished copying the address, Mrs. Williams had left.

"Eleanor, I hate to ask this of you. You have so much of your own work to do. But could you maybe keep an ear up for customers?" Mr. Carvelli asked. "Just until the girls come in? Rosemary called in sick and Angela, she's off to her classes this morning. You have too much of your own work to do, but if you don't mind . . ."

"Mr. Carvelli, of course I'll keep an ear up. Anything."

At lunchtime, Eleanor waited on customers at the soda fountain. She served the one thing she could actually cook —

grilled cheese. Not one person complained. And not one person got up and left, either, after learning of the limited menu. In a glass at the end of the counter, Eleanor placed the tips people left her. "For Mrs. Williams," she wrote on a sign. She folded the paper so it would stand in front.

Eleanor could hear Clarice and Susan giggling as they headed toward the back of the store. They both poked their heads into the cubby — Clarice first, with her tentative smile, then Susan, her whole face tentative.

"Hi, Eleanor," Clarice said. She turned her head toward the register. "Is Mrs. Williams out back or something?"

"She's probably waiting there with a broom in one hand and a dustpan in the other," Susan said.

Eleanor folded her hands on the desk. Mr. Carvelli should really be the one to tell them. But he would struggle so hard, and his words would come out backwards and sideways. Even Mama had had trouble. *Oh, sweetie, this is so hard. I don't know how to tell you.*

"I have some bad news for you both," Eleanor said. "It's about Michael Williams. He was killed in the Pacific. Mrs. Williams got the news last night."

"Michael!" Clarice dropped into the chair opposite Eleanor. "Oh, my God!" She blessed herself quickly. "Oh, my God!" she said again and burst into tears.

Susan's eyes were wide and frightened. "Michael Williams? But we know him. I mean, we didn't know him very well because he's older . . . he *was* older." She stopped talking suddenly and put her hand to her mouth.

Then, just like the mechanical woodsman Eleanor had as a little girl, Susan started in again, her words chopping away until they finally sputtered to a halt. "Oh, God. Poor Mrs. Williams. What will she do? Michael's her whole life. I mean, I complain about her sometimes. When she tells me to dust the shelves and I have a million other things to do. Because she's like a second mother, and I have trouble enough with my first one. But I don't really mind. I don't. Really!"

Clarice brushed the tears from her face. Then she reached her hand across the desk and patted Susan's hand. "You're really very nice to her — all the time. And we'll go to the wake. If they have a wake. I don't know what they do for soldiers or sailors." Both heads swiveled toward Eleanor.

"I'll find out," Eleanor told them. She picked up a pencil and began scribbling on the desk blotter. *Ask somebody about wake,* she wrote.

"Michael was her whole life. What will she do?" Susan asked.

"I don't know."

Daddy and Mrs. Williams and Mama and her scarred face — the images flashed through Eleanor's mind like a newsreel at the Rialto. For a whole year and a half now, she had been crying and complaining and pouting every minute of every hour, feeling oh-so-sorry for herself. Poor little Eleanor. *I can't take this. I hate you, God, for being so mean to me.*

But what about Mama? What about Grams? What about Daddy's patients? No other doctor could read people's eyes the way Daddy could. What about Mary, his nurse, who kept a box of chocolates in her desk just for Daddy? What about the people in the bakery where he got his coffee and jelly doughnut every morning? And what about her friends? Eleanor had abandoned Marybeth and every other friend after the fire. She hadn't wanted any of them to see her face. She never imagined they might actually need her — the way she needed Mrs. Williams.

When Daddy's wake was held, Eleanor still lay in the hospital, wrapped in gauze. Afterward, the bandages made it easy for her to pretend to be sleeping while Mama told her every detail. "You should have seen all the people. Even Mike Stanton, the butcher. And Marge and Jerry Sampson, all the way from Albany. Imagine." Her voice sounded scratchy.

Enough, Mama. I don't want to hear any more. Eleanor tried not to think about Mama and Lindy at the wake, sitting like islands in their grief while bubbles of laughter broke all around them.

Mama kept on talking, and the scratchiness in her voice got worse. "Everyone was telling stories about Daddy. Funny stories mostly, but some were about how he had helped them. It made me so proud." She stopped talking then and cleared her throat a few times. Her voice was Mama's again when she whispered, "Good night, sweetie. Sleep tight. Don't let the bedbugs bite."

But people weren't laughing or telling stories at Michael Williams's wake when Eleanor and Mr. and Mrs. Carvelli walked up the front steps. The people on the porch stood in silence or whispered as though they were saying prayers inside a church. Mrs. Williams' brother stood in the front entry of the Williams's house, shaking hands and greeting everyone who entered. A big man, he hunched his shoulders and back so he could kiss each woman's cheek and shake each man's hand.

Mrs. Carvelli gave him the casserole she'd baked that afternoon. She bustled her way through the Gold Star Mothers who stood in the front hall and showed photographs of their dead sons, past the Sodality women and two priests who prayed the rosary by a pair of French doors, into the Williams's living room. She sat heavily on the sofa next to Mrs. Williams and took hold of one of the woman's hands, patting it vigorously. "You poor, poor woman, losing your baby like that. I don't know how you can even be breathing. Nothing left to live for, I bet you're thinking." The sea of Irish faces around her looked shocked. Eleanor was sure they had all been telling Mrs. Williams that life goes on and so would she. Mrs. Williams's face crumpled a bit. When she saw Eleanor, it collapsed entirely. She gathered Eleanor into her arms and sobbed.

Squeezed against Mrs. Williams's chest, Eleanor could hardly breathe. She had to pull her head away and take huge gulps of air. Mrs. Carvelli stood to one side, blabbing to a woman who was holding a plate of cookies. "Like I said to Chubbs last night, this war's a total disaster. Disaster, I'm telling you. Killing off boys like Michael here. Making everybody crazy with grief." Mr. Carvelli stood next to his wife, his hands folded neatly in front of him. His eyes carried the sadness of the entire world.

Seeing all the faces, with their mouths opening and shutting, forming words she couldn't hear, gave Eleanor a headache. She focused her eyes on the bay window instead, where a photograph sat on an easel. A small card attached to the easel said simply, "Michael Williams, 1924–1944."

What a child he seemed, all dressed up in a graduation cap and gown, just a thin boy with big ears and a shy smile. He looked like a skinnier, fairer-skinned version of Robert. *Robert.* Suddenly, Eleanor's eyes no longer focused. "I have to go out for a minute," she said, but Mrs. Williams's arms were too tightly wrapped around her. "I really think I have to get out of here," Eleanor said a little louder. The room had begun to spin. In another minute, her knees would be too weak to support her.

A hand touched her shoulder. "Come, Eleanor. Maybe we should get a breath of fresh air. That way other people can pay their respects, too."

Eleanor's knees shook as Mr. Carvelli guided her through the living room and the hall, out to the glider on the back porch. "You sit right down here right beside me, Eleanor," he said. "You're not looking so good. You want someone to take you home?"

"It's just — too much."

"Too much," he said, and nodded. "That I understand."

Robert, Robert, Robert. With his little white dog and his beautiful eyes and his "You should be a writer, Eleanor." "It's just Michael and seeing his picture like that and thinking the whole while . . ."

For the longest time, they sat on the glider and swayed

gently back and forth. "And I'm thinking all the time about Robert," Eleanor said finally.

Mr. Carvelli had big hands for such a small man. They rested against his chest, then his knees, then wandered back to his chest again. "Robert is your friend?"

"Robert is . . . a soldier I've been writing to. He'll be going overseas soon. I don't want him to go. I don't want anything bad to happen to him — the way it happened to Michael Williams." The words tumbled out before Eleanor could polish them in her head.

"You don't worry anymore about your Robert," Mr. Carvelli said. "He will be just fine. He'll come home all in one piece. You'll see. Before you know it, he will walk down Everett Street waving to you. 'Hello, Eleanor. I'm home.'"

Eleanor's eyes filled with tears. She tried blinking them away. She tried holding her chin perfectly still. But the tears spilled onto her cheeks, and suddenly she was crying harder than she had ever cried in her entire life, crying so hard that she could feel sharp pains inside her chest.

Mr. Carvelli patted her back and shoulder. He took one of her hands and held on. "Eleanor, please. What can I say to you? What can I do?"

Poor Mr. Carvelli. She hiccupped a little, hearing the bewilderment in his voice. It helped her begin breathing again. "Nothing," she managed to whisper. "There's nothing anyone can do."

Mr. Carvelli was still holding onto her hand. He had placed a handkerchief in her lap. "I'm sorry," she said. "I'm really sorry."

"You go right ahead and cry, Eleanor. You have lots of

things to cry about. I'll just sit here beside you, make sure you are all right."

She blurted out the words the way she would have blurted them out to Daddy. "Robert doesn't know. I couldn't tell him. Not now. Not yet." Her voice didn't work properly. "How could I tell him about *this*?" She touched her face and let her fingers slide down her cheek to her neck.

"Oh, Eleanor . . ." Mr. Carvelli shook her hand gently. "So much I need to say. But finding the right words, it is very hard." She had heard him at the drugstore sometimes, saying to himself, "I need to figure out how to do this" when some doctor had sent in a complicated prescription.

"Your scars," he said finally. "They are just scars on the outside. Inside, you are so many special things. My Angela and me, we pretend sometimes. 'That's our Eleanor,' we say. 'She works so hard. She helps her mama so much. She makes us proud.'" He squeezed her hand. "This Robert. He knows you, Eleanor. He has your letters. You are special to him, too. When he finds out about your face, it won't matter."

Why couldn't everyone see with Mr. Carvelli's eyes. Why couldn't she? Why couldn't Robert? Maybe he would, if she gave him the chance. Maybe others would, too. Her eyes began to fill again. This time, she willed the tears away. Mr. Carvelli's handkerchief was soaked enough. But when she tried to hand it back to him, he folded his hands around hers.

"You keep it. A gift to you."

Mama was alone in the kitchen when Eleanor arrived home. She had one of Lindy's dresses stretched on the table in front of her, and she was actually sewing along the bottom edge. Every time she took a stitch, she inspected it and then nodded as if to say, "Well done." She looked like a little girl, her hair falling into her eyes, the tip of her tongue just showing between parted teeth.

Eleanor sat in the chair opposite Mama. "What are you doing?"

"Practicing my hemming. Are you hungry? Just let me get this ironed and I'll fix you a snack." She snapped the thread and pushed the needle into the collar of her blouse.

"You iron, Mama. I'll cook. Mr. Carvelli said my grilled cheese sandwiches aren't half bad. Not even one burned mark. They're better than my driving, anyway."

Mama laughed, a bit too loudly. "Lindy's sound asleep. She wanted me to play dolls with her, but I begged off. I just wasn't in the mood." Her hands fidgeted with the sleeves of the dress. "I'm sorry I didn't go to the wake with you, Eleanor. There are some things I just can't bring myself to do yet."

"It's all right, Mama. You didn't even know Mrs. Williams, except through me."

"Oh, sweetie. I try to be strong, but sometimes . . ." She gave a weak little smile. "Sometimes the memories are just too much. I hope you understand."

Eleanor took one of Mama's hands and pressed it to her lips. "I understand, Mama. I had to go. For Mrs. Williams. No — for me. Besides, Mr. and Mrs. Carvelli were there the whole time. They even walked me home afterward. Mr. Carvelli's so nice."

July 18, 1944

Dear Robert,

    *We have had awful news. I told you about Mrs. Williams —
the woman who pretty much runs Carvelli's? Well, her son
was killed in the Pacific. I can't believe it yet. She was always
talking about him. "My Michael this and my Michael that."*

    *I went to the wake tonight. I wanted to say something,
anything, to comfort her. But I just couldn't think of the right
words. People always say things like, "God wanted an angel
in Heaven, so He took your son . . ." Or daughter or mother
or father. Whoever. That doesn't seem very comforting to me.
But then, thinking about God isn't all that comforting. I get so
angry at Him sometimes. So many bad things happen in this
world, like war and people getting hurt and killed. I'm not
sure I want to be on a first-name basis with someone who
allows such things to happen.*

    *I haven't been to a lot of wakes, so I was nervous. But Mr.
Carvelli took good care of me. He always treats me as if I
were made of the finest china. He treats everyone that way.
Mama says it's the mark of a true gentleman.*

    *I'm ashamed to tell you this. Last spring, after we
moved to Beachmont, I would have died if any of my
friends saw me with Mr. Carvelli. He's so old-fashioned
with his black suit and hat. Now, mornings when I'm
working, we walk to the drugstore together. He checks to
make sure there is no traffic before he allows me to cross
the street, then he takes my elbow as we step off the curb.
If Mama or Mrs. Carvelli did the same thing, I would want
to strangle them. But with Mr. Carvelli, it's as if my father*

were looking down from Heaven and decided to send this kind little man to protect me.

When I was a little girl, I used to look up at the stars and think, "That's where heaven is." I still like to imagine my father sitting up there on his own personal star. I never had the chance to say good-bye to him, and I keep thinking that if only I knew what star he was on, I could wave to him or something.

Everywhere we go, ads and entertainers are telling us to make sure we cheer up the boys in uniform. I have a feeling I cheer you down sometimes instead.

I hope you don't think I am a bad person for what I have written.

Please stay safe.

> *Affectionately yours,*
> *Eleanor*

P.S. You never asked me how my father died. It's time I explained. He was killed in a fire. I should have told you that when I wrote about the man who had been burned.

Chapter Twelve

❧ ❧

Without Mrs. Williams to watch over things, the drugstore bumped uncomfortably along. The Friday after Michael died, Mr. Carvelli observed, "The floor looks a little dusty." He said the words as if he were apologizing.

Eleanor looked at the puffs of dust gathering under the soda fountain and in the corners of the display shelves. Then she looked at the stacks of prescriptions piled on her desk. She sighed. "I'll get to it right away."

Mr. Carvelli poked his head into her cubby. "Not you, Eleanor. You do everything around here lately. You have become the chief cashier, the chief stocker of shelves, even the chief cook and bottlewasher at lunchtime."

"Mr. Carvelli, if I ever really become the chief cook around here, you're in big trouble. The only thing I haven't burned is water."

His white teeth sparkled when he grinned at her. "You shouldn't have to worry your head about burning things. Or cleaning, either." The grin disappeared. "Other people should be taking care of such things."

Other people meant Rosemary.

Eleanor pushed the prescriptions to one side and stood. Taking dust mop in hand, she marched out to the soda fountain.

Rosemary was humming "A Tisket, a Tasket" while she swished a wet rag across the chrome on the stools.

"Maybe you could clean underneath the display cases," Eleanor announced. She struggled to keep her tone even. "And the floor hasn't been mopped for a week now."

"I'll get to it," Rosemary said. She didn't reach for the dust mop. Instead, she floated to the perfume display. She sampled each fragrance as she placed bottles of L'Air du Temps on top of the glass case. "We have some mighty pretty smells in this place, you know that, Eleanor?"

Even the tips of Eleanor's fingers prickled with anger. "We have some mighty lazy *people* in this place." The words skipped around Eleanor's tongue. They escaped as a mumble that Rosemary ignored. "I have to visit the little girl's room," she said as she drifted toward the back room.

Eleanor marched back into the cubby. Her body landed in the chair with a thud. The summer before last, she wouldn't have mumbled her words like some scared rabbit. She would have shouted them into Rosemary's ear.

Sister Agnes had once lectured Eleanor's religion class. "Hell isn't what you think it is," she had advised. "It's not a place of fire and brimstone where you burn for eternity. Imagine the worst fear you have and multiply it a hundred times, a thousand times. Then think about living with that fear every second of every day for eternity. That's what Hell is."

Eleanor and her friends had giggled about Hell at lunchtime. "My biggest fear is that I'll be stuck in Sister Thomas Michael's algebra class forever," Marybeth said. "And if I flunk any more of her tests, it might really happen."

"I thought your biggest fear was appearing in public without lipstick," Eleanor teased her.

Everyone sitting at the table laughed. Everyone talked about being afraid. Except Eleanor. "I can't imagine anything worse than the Hell they talk about in the Bible," she said.

"That's because you're not afraid of anything," Marie Macklin said. Marie was round and short, and she blushed every time anyone spoke to her.

Marybeth had placed her arm around Eleanor's shoulder. "That's true," she said. "My friend, Eleanor the Fearless."

But Eleanor wasn't fearless anymore. Every day those people storms raged around her, pressing her deeper and deeper into the shadows. She hated the way she had become afraid to speak what was on her mind. Every time she opened her mouth, she edited her words. *Be nice, Eleanor. Say kind things. If you're nice enough to people, they will be nice to you.*

Her eyes rested on Robert's initials. Robert could help her escape from those shadows. She could be Eleanor the Fearless again, if she could just trust him enough to tell him the truth.

A voice called out from the middle of the store. "Didn't anyone clean a single thing while I was gone? We could breed dust bunnies under the perfume counter!"

The shadows pressing on Eleanor retreated. She jumped

160

out of her chair and hurried toward the center aisle. "Mrs. Williams! It's so wonderful to see you."

For an instant, joy flashed in Mrs. Williams's eyes. She opened her arms, and Eleanor stepped into them. "It's wonderful to see you, too," Mrs. Williams said. "When I woke up this morning, I asked myself, 'What do you need most?' And I answered, 'Carvelli's. I need to go to work again. I need to be with Chubbs and Eleanor and all my customers again.'"

She released Eleanor suddenly. Her hand cupped Eleanor's chin. "And you know what? I was right. I can't tell you how happy I am to be here."

Her happiness lasted less than a minute. That's when she spotted the L'Air du Temps bottles on top of the display case. That's when Rosemary drifted back toward the perfume counter.

Rosemary was babbling. "I'm thinking. Get a few more of those fancy bottles up on top, so's people can see them." She jolted to a stop when she spotted Mrs. Williams. "You're back."

Mrs. Williams didn't even say hello. She muttered to herself as she shifted the perfume bottles from the top of the case to the shelf beneath. "I don't know how many times you have to explain things to *some* people. Cheap perfume goes on top of the case. Expensive perfume goes inside. Anyone with half a brain knows you keep the good stuff under lock and key so it won't disappear like yesterday's trash."

And she wasn't finished complaining. Right before lunch, while Eleanor sat cross-legged on the floor, sorting through a box from Purington's Medical Supplies, Mrs. Williams stood in front of the soda fountain grill. In a voice that could have split granite, she asked, "I got out of bed to face *this* mess?"

She used the same tone with poor Will Richardson. Will made the mistake of taking a bottle of cough syrup out of Eleanor's hands before she placed it on the shelf in front of the register. "I suppose you think you're going to charge that," Mrs. Williams growled. "You keep saying you're gonna pay off that bill of yours, but I haven't seen a cent of your money."

Will's face flushed. He handed the bottle of syrup to Eleanor and stalked out of the drugstore without saying a word.

Two tiny boys burst through the front door. A woman, carrying a toddler on one hip, followed them. She shifted the toddler to her other hip before plodding toward the counter. "Don't you touch anything," she told the boys, who were already poking fingers and noses into every box within their reach.

Eleanor grabbed a bottle of Shire's Liniment before it toppled to the floor. Mrs. Williams tried smiling, first at Eleanor and then at the woman. The woman smiled back. "You got some kind of energy pills? Something to either kill theirs or build up mine?" She grabbed the smallest boy by the collar just as he motored into the aspirin display in front of the register. Bottles flew across the center aisle. "Didn't I tell you not to touch anything, Michael?" she scolded.

Mrs. Williams stiffened. The smile she had planted on her mouth disappeared. In that stone-cold voice, she said, "People who can't handle children shouldn't have them."

The woman yanked her sons, screaming and kicking, down the aisle and out of the drugstore. The door slammed behind her.

"Mrs. Williams shouldn't have come back so soon," Rosemary whispered as she dropped coins into the cash register drawer. "We won't have a single customer left, the way she keeps biting their heads off. She's not doing *anybody* any good by being here."

Eleanor was still replacing aspirin bottles on the shelves. "She's not the only one not doing anybody any good." Eleanor actually said the words out loud, but Rosemary was still too busy talking to hear her.

"The change is from yesterday," Rosemary explained. Eleanor could barely make out her words. "I rang up Ed's sandwich, but I forgot to put the money in the drawer. I just shoved it in my pocket. It was such a zoo in here. Remember? I hope Mrs. Williams doesn't hear about it, or she'll have my head."

But Mrs. Williams had radar for ears. She had heard every word, and she exploded. "You *forgot*? You're not that stupid, Rosemary. Incompetent, maybe. And I refuse to put up with your incompetence any longer. You're robbing Chubbs blind! I checked the slips from yesterday." She stomped over to the register. Pushing Rosemary aside, she punched open the drawer and flung the register slips onto the counter. "See that?" Her fingers pointed at the slips and then at Rosemary. "Seventy-three cents short. Twenty-one cents the day before. Ninety-four cents in all. Did you think I wouldn't notice?"

Mr. Carvelli stopped in the middle of explaining a medication to a customer and rushed to the counter. "Mrs. Williams. Please," he said.

But Mrs. Williams wasn't listening. "You make me sick,

you know that, Rosemary?" she screamed. "You don't care about anything, do you? You don't care how hard everyone has to work just to make up for your laziness."

Rosemary gulped back tears.

Eleanor placed one hand over the slips on the counter. Her other hand rested on Mrs. Williams's shoulder. "Mrs. Williams, you have to stop this. Anyone could have made the mistake, not just Rosemary. And it *was* busy at lunchtime. Please. I'll put the money in myself."

Mrs. Williams collapsed in stages. First her arms dropped to her sides, then her knees buckled. Eleanor and Mr. Carvelli each took one of her arms and helped her into the cubby. She fell into Eleanor's chair.

"I'm sorry," she said. "I'm sorry, I'm sorry, I'm sorry." She lifted a tear-stained face. Her eyes focused only on Eleanor. "It's just too much to handle."

"I will call a taxi to take you home," Mr. Carvelli said. He disappeared behind the counter.

"They tell me I should talk about him. They say I should keep Michael's things out, so I remember him. 'That way it'll be like he's still alive,' they say. But they don't know anything, Eleanor. He *is* dead, and I think I'm dying, too." She grasped Eleanor's hand. "You understand how I feel, don't you, honey. I know you do. Because of your father."

Eleanor was drowning. She struggled to keep her head above the pools of sorrow in Mrs. Williams's eyes. "I do understand, Mrs. Williams. Sometimes it's just too hard for . . ." Her throat closed before she could finish the sentence.

Rosemary stood in the doorway to the cubby. "We all understand," she said. She took a step closer to Mrs. Williams's chair. "It takes time. Michael's been dead, what — barely a week? You gotta stop trying to take care of things here. You gotta go home and take care of you."

Mrs. Williams's head bobbed up and down like the nodding doll on Mama's bureau. "That is what I need to do — take care of myself." Her face turned toward Eleanor's. In a child's tiny voice, she whispered, "But when does the pain go away? Tell me the truth, Eleanor. Because I can't stand this. I feel like I'm bleeding from a thousand wounds all at once. And I'm afraid I'll never stop."

A car horn beeped twice. A man wearing the blue uniform of Babson's Cab Service pushed through the front door. Eleanor squeezed Mrs. Williams's hand, then released it. "That's your taxi, Mrs. Williams. You need to go home now." Mr. Carvelli walked Mrs. Williams out the door and helped her into the cab.

The whole store relaxed when the taxi pulled away. Rosemary leaned her shoulder against the cubby doorway. "I gotta tell you, Eleanor. That must be what they mean by grief making you crazy."

Rosemary *was* stupid. *It's not grief that makes you crazy. It's fear. Who would ever need Mrs. Williams the way Michael had? And who would ever need Eleanor at all?*

Robert! All the way home, Eleanor could imagine the touch of his hand on her face. Ridiculous. But when she stepped off the streetcar at the corner of Everett Street, his presence felt so real that she checked in both directions for a soldier with a little boy smile and long eyelashes.

She searched the Carvellis' walkway, the steps, the front porch. But the only person waiting on the porch was Lindy. "What are you looking for, Ellie?" she asked. She didn't wait for an answer. "Mrs. Carvelli made me another dress for my doll!"

Eleanor sat on the step beside Lindy. "Did anyone come while I was gone?"

"Nobody except Mr. Partenope. He was just bringing the mail. Mrs. Carvelli and he talked and talked and talked. About soldiers and stuff. And about you getting letters from Robert."

The air grew suddenly cold. "What *about* me getting letters from Robert?"

Lindy shrugged. "They were just talking about him and you being friends. I told them he wasn't just any friend. He was a boyfriend."

"Whatever happened to, 'I promise, Eleanor?'"

Lindy shook her head.

"You blab my secret all over town and now you won't even tell me why?"

"I didn't tell anyone else. Not even Jeannie when she told me about her sister getting married." Lindy's voice had that teary sound to it. "Not even when she said you'd never have a boyfriend." The teary sound was full-blown now, accompanied by shaking shoulders and a runny nose that Lindy wiped on her sleeve.

Of course. In Lindy's Cinderella world, her big sister was supposed to be the beautiful princess who married Prince

Charming. But now that world had popped. Poor Lindy. It must be terrible to have to grow up so suddenly.

Eleanor wrapped one arm around Lindy's shoulder. "It's all right," she said. "You don't have to cry. I understand."

Besides, she didn't really care anymore if Lindy announced Robert's existence to everyone on Everett Street, or to everyone in Beachmont. Robert *was* Eleanor's boyfriend, not somebody she created out of letters.

She scanned the street. No khaki-colored uniform. No uncertain face checking houses for a familiar number. The man in the corner house trimmed the roses in his side yard and when he looked up, just for a moment, Eleanor smiled at him.

Lindy fidgeted against Eleanor's arm. "You're squashing me," she complained between sniffles. "I have to get something out of my pocket. I know you'll like it."

The world was suddenly a blur of pink and green and blue, and every color of the rainbow besides. "Do you have a letter for me, Lindy?"

"Maybe," Lindy giggled.

"Did you open my letter?" Eleanor asked. "Did you stand on top of the roof and read my letter out loud to everyone in the entire city? Did you send it off to WBZ, so they could read my letter on the air?"

Lindy giggled again. "No."

"Then give it to me, please. And then you'd better wash your face. You have streaks of dirt all down your cheeks. If Mrs. Carvelli sees you, she'll think we've run out of soap."

Lindy rummaged through her pocket. "It's with the other letters I was supposed to give to Mama. But I forgot."

Two yellow envelopes dropped onto Eleanor's lap. Bills again. The third one, with its red-and-blue border, landed on the step beside her. *Robert!*

The flap on Robert's envelope tempted her. She wanted so much to poke her finger under it and take one tiny peek. But she folded her hands and placed them on her lap instead. She didn't want to read Robert's letter. Not yet. Not with Lindy sitting beside her, all prepared to smile.

But Lindy surprised her. "I have to go now. Mrs. Carvelli's teaching Mama how to sew. I want to learn, too."

Eleanor waited until Lindy disappeared into the house. *Robert, Robert, Robert.* The words sang inside her head as she took Robert's letter out of its envelope. Just before she read his words, she had an awful thought. What if Mrs. Williams received letters from Michael after his death? It happened sometimes. Telegrams always traveled faster than the mail. What would it do to her to see Michael's handwriting — to think, just for an instant, that he was alive after all? Eleanor would die if that ever happened to her.

July 20, 1944

Dear Eleanor,

I'm sorry to hear about Mrs. Williams's son. However, you and her other friends will be of great comfort to her, the same way your family and friends must have comforted you when your father died.

I had wondered about his death. Perhaps I should have guessed something when you wrote about the man who had been burned.

Eleanor, you are not a bad person for questioning God. Sometimes I wonder about Him, too. It is only natural in times like these.

I like your idea about Heaven. Just last night, I was looking up at the sky. "Eleanor's father is up there somewhere, looking down on her and on me, too." I thought, "Nice to meet you, Mr. Driscoll. My name is Robert Bettencourt, and I am a friend of your daughter's."

Do you know what I think, Eleanor? I think you just pick a star. Any star. Then you tell him how you feel.

Tonight, when you look up, I'll be looking at the same stars and thinking about you.

Take care of yourself, Eleanor.

> *Affectionately yours,*
> *Robert*

Chapter Thirteen

❧ ❧

July 22, 1944

Dear Robert,

Your letter arrived this afternoon.

I should have explained right away about my father. But I have a hard time talking about the fire. Mama still reads every detail she can find in the newspaper. I would rather forget. Not forget Daddy, of course, but what took him away from us. What you said about my father and the stars? I can't tell you how much that meant to me.

I have to tell you something else, though. I'm actually going to try another driving lesson. Clarice called ten minutes ago and asked if next Saturday morning at eight was a good time for me.

I'm not sure any time is a good time for me to be behind a steering wheel. Maybe two in the morning, when there's not a soul on the road, but even then there are trees and bushes that might want to commit plant suicide by jumping in front of the car.

But Clarice has those puppy-dog eyes I just can't resist.

She was calling on the phone, so I couldn't actually see those puppy-dog eyes, but I could imagine them.

If you hear of a four-hundred-car pile-up in the Boston area, don't be surprised. I promise to write the second I get home from the lesson, so I can tell you all the details.

Robert, thank you again for what you said about the stars and my father. I did go out last night and look up at the sky. And I wondered, "Did Robert choose the same star I did?"

Please stay safe.

                                        Affectionately yours,
                                        Eleanor

P.S. The other day, Mr. Carvelli was teaching his wife how to parallel park. She pulled their Buick between two cars, slick as you please. Mr. Carvelli sat in the passenger seat, and he didn't even look scared! Life is full of surprises.

Early Saturday morning, Eleanor mailed the letter at the tiny branch post office by Immaculate Conception Church. She listened for the *plink* as the envelope slipped through the slot marked "Out of Town" and landed on top of whatever letters were already in the bin. *Travel safely, little letter.* She tapped the wall next to the slot. *Tell all your friends that you're special, because you belong to Robert Bettencourt.*

Lots of other girls wrote to soldiers far away. But she would bet a million dollars — well, at least her week's salary — that their soldiers didn't write about stars and Shirley Temple and dreams the way Robert did.

She jumped off the post office stairs, one at a time. *Robert, Robert, Robert.* The traffic policeman stopped the cars just so she could cross the street. The muscles in her cheek didn't even feel tight when she smiled at him. He smiled right back at her, without blinking once. As she walked along, her fingers touched each pleat across the front of her blouse. *He loves me. He loves me not.* They stopped when she reached the last pleat. *Robert loves me.* Of course he did. He wrote all those lovely letters, didn't he?

Eleanor turned the corner onto Ocean Avenue. Someone had chalked a hopscotch game on the sidewalk, and she hopped in each block. She pretended that she was picking up a stone in the far corner. *Hop. Hop. Hop. Robert!*

Her joy lasted until she arrived at the Point. A whole army of boys climbed over the boulders, wrestling, tumbling, howling to each other. They acted like the tiger cubs she and Daddy had seen at the Franklin Park Zoo the day after Lindy was born. "Giant kittens," Eleanor had told him.

"Dangerous kittens," Daddy reminded her.

But Eleanor hadn't understood *dangerous* then the way she did now. Her muscles tensed. How dare the boy army invade her beach today! She was supposed to meet Clarice and Tony here for her driving lesson. Susan, too.

She scraped pebbles from the wall's surface, just in case one of the invaders came within throwing distance. But the boys were too busy pushing and shoving each other to notice her.

"Water rat! I see one. He's huge!" one of the boys shouted. He pointed toward the pier, and suddenly the boys were off, scrambling back over the rocks until they disappeared around the curve of the beach.

Eleanor scattered the pebbles on the sand. Good thing!

These boys had no understanding of the basic rule of Mahoney's Point. They could have the whole beach to themselves every other day of the year, but nights and cold, drizzly days like today belonged to her. Her and Robert.

Someday, he would walk right down Ocean Avenue and out onto the seawall. She would be sitting here, the way she was now. In his crisp uniform, with worry lines around his eyes that hadn't been there in his picture, Eleanor would not recognize him at first.

"Excuse me. Are you Eleanor? Eleanor Driscoll?"

She would turn toward him. And he would see her face.

His eyes would widen at first. They might even dart away and look up at the clouds or toward the sand. But soon enough, his eyes would return to her face. And they would soften, as if he were gazing at someone precious to him. "Eleanor. It's so good to finally meet you."

From the street behind the seawall, a car honked three times. *Tony.* Eleanor brushed the sand off her skirt and stood. But she couldn't abandon her fantasy so suddenly. "It's nice to meet you too, Robert."

Tony leaned on the horn again. "Eleanor, are you coming or not?" His voice carried through the bushes. She almost called back, "You go on without me," but she couldn't abandon Clarice that way. Clarice would sit in the back seat, shyly admiring Tony while Susan pried and pushed him into paying attention to her.

But no Susan glared at Eleanor from the front passenger seat. Clarice sat there instead, wearing a grin on her face as wide as the ocean.

"Susan called to say she felt sick."

Tony opened the front door, and Clarice hopped out of the car. "You sit in the front, Eleanor," she said.

Eleanor hesitated. "No, it's all right. I'll take the back." She looked again at Clarice's glowing face. *She's pretty. She's really pretty.* "You know what? This is turning out to be a bad day for me. Mama's got a list of chores a mile long. You don't mind if I take a raincheck, do you?" She scuffed her feet on the pavement. "I mean, the way things are going, my mind is so occupied that I wouldn't be able to concentrate, anyway. And you know how badly I drive even when I *am* concentrating."

Tony's and Clarice's words collided.

"Come along just for the ride. Please, Eleanor?" Clarice begged.

"You don't drive that badly, Eleanor. It's just a matter of practice," Tony said.

Eleanor heard their voices, but mostly she watched Clarice's face. She recognized that *he loves me, he loves me not* look. "Another time," she said. "I promise."

Tony's eyes searched Eleanor's face. It was hard not to respond to those eyes, because they were so gentle, so accepting. But she turned her head toward the beach roses.

"Some other time, then," Tony said finally. He held the driver's door for Clarice, who hopped in, but not before she smiled at Eleanor. "You are the best human being that ever lived," her smile said, as clearly as if she had shouted it to the whole city.

Tony had already begun explaining. "If you're going to drive a car, you need to know how to start it. First, you put your left foot on that pedal there. The clutch." He lifted his head and saluted Eleanor with his hand. The he turned back toward Clarice.

"Have a good time," Eleanor said as she watched the car lurch down the street. They would laugh and talk about people they knew from the drugstore and buy slush someplace along Ocean Avenue and slurp it in the car while Tony drove Clarice home. And it hurt Eleanor just a little. Because Tony liked her. Eleanor could tell. And nobody had liked her that way for a long time. Except for Robert.

Mrs. Carvelli pounced the minute Eleanor walked up the front steps. "Hey, Eleanor! You should be congratulating me all over the place. You see this piece of paper?" She waved it across Eleanor's face like a child waving a flag on the Fourth of July.

"You got your license?"

Mrs. Carvelli fanned the air once more. "Of course I did. That big, fancy registry man? I told him right in the beginning, 'You are riding with the best driver in Beachmont.' My sister, she took me there. She says, 'You shouldn't oughta brag like that, Angela' but hey, it's not bragging when it's true. That fancy guy tried tricking me on some of those questions, and he made me park the car on the boulevard. Nobody told me I'd have to do that. But when I finished, he said I got my license. 'You ever seen such a good driver?' I asked him. It took him about ten minutes to smile!"

Eleanor's smile didn't take ten minutes to appear. She

could just imagine the scene — Mrs. Carvelli chattering away to the registry official while her sister cringed in the back seat.

"Congratulations, Mrs. Carvelli. You must be proud."

"Don't you worry, Eleanor. You'll catch on. Just have to practice more." She slapped her forehead with her hand. "Oh, sheesh. I almost forgot. I'm supposed to tell you. Your mother, she left you a note on the kitchen table, in case you got home before she did. She and Lindy took the train to Lynn. There's a sale at Loehmann's on fabric."

"Fabric? *Mama?*"

"Well, of course. Your sister's growing out of everything on earth that she owns. It's lots cheaper to make clothes than buy them."

"Did the note say anything else?"

"What do you think I am, a Mrs. Buttinsky or something? I don't read other people's stuff."

"Of course not, Mrs. Carvelli. We know that. And congratulations again. Mr. Carvelli will have to take you someplace ritzy to celebrate."

"Well, sure. It's not every day I get my license."

Mama's note lay on the kitchen table. *Eleanor, Lindy and I have gone to Lynn to buy fabric and a couple of dress patterns. Hope all went well with your driving lesson. We should be home by lunchtime. I love you. Mama.*

How the world could turn upside down in a short time. Mama actually sewing, Mrs. Carvelli with her license, Clarice off with Tony — and Eleanor? *Eleanor Driscoll, reporting from the home front. Today in Beachmont, Massachusetts, the ordinary lives of ordinary people became "such stuff as dreams are made of . . ."*

A red-and-blue corner under Mama's note caught her eye. *Robert! An actual letter from Robert!* A real, honest-to-goodness letter that she could hug to her chest. A song had been playing over and over inside her head for days. *I'll be seeing you in all the old familiar places,* it began. She sang, and her body began to sway with the music. "I'll see you in the morning sun and when my life is through, I'll be looking at the moon but I'll be seeing you."

A door slammed somewhere downstairs, and Mrs. Carvelli's voice carried right up through the open windows. "Hey, Mrs. Sullivan! You hear about me getting my license?"

Eleanor shook her head. Good thing Mrs. Carvelli didn't see Eleanor waltzing around the kitchen all by herself. "That Driscoll girl? I'm telling you. She's gone nuts." And maybe Eleanor was nuts. *Hopeless. I'm completely hopeless, the way I'm acting.* Because she couldn't open the letter right away. She stared at the writing on the envelope until her eyes got blurry. But even with blurry eyes, she could still recognize *Eleanor P. Driscoll.*

July 21, 1944

Dear Eleanor,

I wanted to meet you. I wanted to listen to Mrs. Carvelli go on and on about how she would run the world if she were president. I wanted to listen to Lindy talk about her dolls. I wanted to teach you how to drive, so you would always have the freedom you crave. Most of all, I wanted to sit with you at Mahoney's Point and watch the stars come out.

That's not possible now. By the time you read this letter, I will be on a ship headed for France.

I've been on a boat once before. We took a ferry ride across Lake Champlain when I was eight. My stomach still gets queasy when I think about it. So I'm not looking forward to this journey.

Getting seasick is not my greatest fear, however. Eleanor, I lie to my parents sometimes. I tell them how happy I am to be serving our country in time of war. I tell them that I can't wait to join the fighting. They are so proud of me. My mother brags about her "brave son."

Eleanor, you have such a giving heart. I can tell by the way you write about your father and Michael Williams. You are so honest about your feelings. That's why I can't lie to you.

My mother is wrong. I am not brave. I'm afraid of dying before I have the chance to meet you. I'm afraid of disgracing myself by behaving like a coward.

But this is the hardest thing to admit. I'm afraid of having to kill another person. Eleanor, I wasn't one of those football types in high school or college — the guys with the thick necks and girls hanging on each arm. I didn't like the idea of getting beaten up on the field. I also didn't like the idea of beating up other guys.

But I don't think I'm that different from every other soldier who is in this war. We're not fighting for any great humanitarian reason or to save democracy. We are fighting so the war will end and we can go home again and sit at places like Mahoney's Point and look at the stars with people we love.

I couldn't write about this to anyone else, Eleanor. I hope you will understand.

178

Please write soon. My new address is at the bottom of this page. And please take care of yourself until I come home.

Love,

Robert

This was a gift, wrapped in its military issue envelope. It was so much more precious than the Jo doll she had received from Grams on her tenth birthday. Grams had always given Eleanor clothing before — dresses and blouses with matching skirts. But not this time. This time she had said, "I know how much you loved *Little Women*."

Eleanor could still see the wrapping paper with its pink flowers, still hear the crinkle of the tissue paper as she lifted the doll out of its blue box. She could still smell the doll's newness. She hadn't been able to speak at first, hadn't even thanked Grams, who hovered over her saying, "Do you like it?"

"I need to show Marybeth," Eleanor had said finally. "She'd want to know."

Now Eleanor thought, *I have to tell Clarice.* She'd want to know.

Somebody loves me. Me!

Me! But not really me.

Liar, liar, liar.

Eleanor couldn't lie anymore. And she couldn't wait to find the right words that would make him understand. If she waited, she would never be able to write to him and tell him what she should have told him a lifetime ago, when she was still just *Affectionately yours* to him.

She wrote the letter four times. She thought she would cry the whole time, but her hands didn't even shake. The fourth time, the pen kept slipping out of her fingers, and her handwriting looked like it belonged to an old person. But she folded the letter anyway and placed it inside an envelope. Then she took it out and read it one last time.

July 24, 1944

Dear Robert,

I do understand, Robert. I would like to have met you, too. It would have been fun to teach you how to skip stones or, as you say, just sit with you at Mahoney's Point and watch the stars come out.

I can't tell you not to be afraid. You have every reason to feel that way. Robert, I am honored to know someone like you. Because I think you are incredibly brave. Real bravery is when you admit you are afraid, but you do things in spite of that.

So I'm going to be brave, too, starting right now. Because I have not been honest with you. I sent you a picture of me that is not really me. That Eleanor doesn't exist anymore.

Daddy was not the only one who died in the fire at the Palm Gardens. I did, too — or at least the girl you saw in the picture did.

We were celebrating my sixteenth birthday, just Daddy and me. We danced. We ate shrimp cocktail. I drank gingerale with grenadine syrup; Daddy drank an old-fashioned. I can remember every detail — the sparkle of the silver trays, the soldiers lined up along the back waiting to dance with girls like me who waltzed across the floor. And the music. Always the music.

I'm not sure how the fire started. I remember screaming. I remember Daddy grabbing my hands and dragging me through the crowd. "You're hurting me, Daddy," I said, but he kept pulling me along. Little bits of flame landed on my face, my neck. "Cover your face!" he shouted. But I couldn't. He had my hands.

I don't remember anything else except the smell. And later, the tags. As we lay on cots in long rows in the hospital corridors, they placed tags on our feet. One color was for dead people. Mine was blue, for those who had been badly burned.

Robert, that's why I'm no longer the girl you see in your picture. I have scars covering half of my face and most of my chest and neck.

I have really liked writing to you all these months. I liked receiving your letters even more. But I will understand if you don't want to write anymore. And I won't hate you, either.

Thank you so much for everything. I'm sorry I'm not the girl you thought I was. I will always think of you fondly, and I hope you can remember me the same way.

Please stay safe.

Love,
Eleanor

Chapter Fourteen

❧ ❧

Mr. Partenope clucked his tongue against the roof of his mouth. "Well, you see, Eleanor, you got the fast transport ships and you got the slow transport ships. The fast ones, they take about ten days to cross the Atlantic. The slow ones take a mite longer. Couple of weeks, maybe. That's if they don't meet up with any of those storms brewing out there in the ocean. It'll be hurricane season soon enough. So you're looking at almost three weeks before a letter actually catches up with someone overseas. Then it's another three weeks or so before you get any mail back."

Six weeks? Eleanor had to clench her teeth to keep from screaming out loud. "Would they — would he — definitely get a letter, though? Even though the address doesn't specifically say France?"

"You mean if you sent it to one of those APO addresses?"

All the breath escaped from Eleanor's lungs at once. "Yes. Like that."

Mr. Partenope's smile spread across his mouth and creased the corners of his eyes. He had dark brown eyes that reminded Eleanor of the "coffee — black, no sugar" that Ed the policeman ordered every time he set foot in the drugstore.

"Let me tell you, Eleanor, we got people moving all over the place," Mr. Partenope explained. "They move from this city to that one, from one country to another. Eventually, we find them all and deliver their mail."

He shifted the mailbag from his left shoulder to his right. "This war," he said, shaking his head. "People getting letters, people sending letters all over the world. I never delivered so many letters to so many people in all my years. I can't help getting fond of all these people, like they're friends or something. 'Don't get so attached, Warren.' That's what the wife says. 'They're just names on an envelope.' But that's not how it is to me."

Drops of sweat gathered in pools under Eleanor's eyes. She closed them, just for a moment. Could the day be any hotter? When she opened them again, her eyelashes clumped together, making it hard for her to see. "Not all the heroes are overseas, Mr. Partenope," she said.

Mr. Partenope's eyes concentrated on his feet. They scuffed along the edges of the walkway, kicking at the pebbles gathered between the cracks. "I got to get going now. I got to finish delivering all those letters. You have a good day, young lady."

Eleanor would have bet any amount of money on God's

green earth that Mr. Partenope walked faster than usual toward the Beauchamps' house. In her mind, she kissed his cheek good-bye.

Three weeks before Robert even received her letter? Six whole weeks before she found out how he felt about it? Eleanor threw herself across her bed and buried her cheek against her pillow.

In six weeks, Eleanor would be dead from worrying. She was dying now. Parts of her had already shut down. In six weeks, if Robert hadn't written, the top story on the *Globe's* front page would read, "Girl Collapses When Soldier Breaks Her Heart." She amended the headline. *Bruises* her heart. Any breaking would be Eleanor's doing. She had inflicted the fractures herself when she sent Robert her picture.

If only she could write the pain away. Eleanor pulled the pillow from under her head and pressed it to her chest. Why couldn't she do that? Why couldn't she write just one more letter to Robert, explaining her last one? She even had the perfect opening: *Dear Robert, I have a news flash for you. The state of Massachusetts actually issued a driver's license to Mrs. Carvelli.* He would have to smile at those words. And then — she squeezed the pillow harder — he would read the rest of her letter, and he would forget her face and he would be friends with her again, the way he was before *Love, Robert* complicated everything.

Eleanor threw the pillow onto the floor and hopped off the bed. *I can do this. I can make him see* Affectionately yours, Eleanor *again*. She reached between the mattress and the box spring and pulled out her stationery, but her trembling fingers made it hard to grasp the pages. They made it even harder for her to fill Daddy's pen before she began writing. The ink splashed onto her bed, leaving droplets of black on the white bedspread.

July 29, 1944

Dear Robert,

I have a news flash for you. The state of Massachusetts actually issued a driver's license to Mrs. Carvelli. The most depressing part of the news is that she actually drives well. Unlike me. My lesson the other day got cancelled. If they knew how bad a driver I really am, everyone one in Beachmont would be grateful

I have sad news to report, too. I didn't tell you in my last letter, but Mrs. Williams returned to work last week. She's hurting so much. She was rude to customers, and that's not like her at all. Then she said really hateful things to Rosemary. I'm not saying that Rosemary is the best employee Mr. Carvelli has ever hired. Most of the time, she makes the witch in Snow White and the Seven Dwarfs seem like Little Mary Sunshine. But even Rosemary has feelings, and Mrs. Williams smashed them to pieces.

I have more to say, but the rest is so much harder.

I disappointed you, Robert. But I hope you will find it in your heart to forgive me and be my friend anyway.

Perhaps it would help if I explained something.

I used to be pretty once — well, almost pretty. I had smooth skin and a dimple in my right cheek. People didn't mind looking at me. I didn't mind looking at me.

After the fire, I didn't look in a mirror for the longest time. I still don't if I can help it. I mean, I check my teeth to see if there's broccoli stuck between them, and I look to make sure my hair is neat, but I don't really see myself. Because it's not just that other people can't stand looking at me. I can't stand looking at me, either.

That's why I sent the picture of me that was taken before the fire. It was just too hard to believe that you would see me, *Eleanor, and not just the scars on my face.*

I don't know if that helps explain anything. I hope it does. Please stay safe.

Her hand poised over the paper. *Yours truly? Affectionately? Affectionately yours?*

Mama and Lindy were talking in the kitchen.

"I want to start school now," Lindy was saying. "I want to learn to write cursive, like Jeannie does. She doesn't have to print like a baby."

Mama's voice held a laughter that hadn't been there for a long while. "School will be starting soon enough, little chick. You'll learn cursive soon enough, and then you'll go off to high school and learn to speak French and study things like algebra and literature. Then, before you know it, you'll be all grown up and leaving the house to get married."

"I want to marry Robert," Lindy said. "If he doesn't marry Eleanor. Do you think he will? Jeannie says Eleanor will never get married. She says Eleanor isn't pretty enough to get married."

Robert's letter lay on the bed in front of Eleanor. She folded it carefully and placed it inside an envelope. She didn't bother addressing the front. Instead, she shoved the envelope under her mattress. *For some other day, Robert. For some day when being pretty isn't as important as being me.*

On the desk blotter in her cubby, Eleanor wrote *Six Weeks!!!!!* She underlined the words. She drew boxes around them.

Rosemary breezed through, dropping her sweater onto the chair beside Eleanor. "I must be some kind of hero, don't you think, Eleanor? For coming back here the day after Mrs. Williams rips me into little shreds in front of the whole universe?" She gave a sigh that reached right down into Eleanor's toes. "I mean, you try to do your best around here, to be helpful, and what do you get? A crazy lady screaming in your eardrums!"

Eleanor's pencil tip scraped against the blotter paper, tearing a hole deep into the pad. "If you really wanted to be helpful," she said, "you would stop gossiping about poor Mrs. Williams and clean the shelves out back, so Mr. Carvelli wouldn't have to dust the pill bottles before he fills them for customers."

Rosemary's mouth opened three times before she spoke. "You don't need to get so huffy about it. All somebody has to do is say something."

Eleanor counted to three. "Somebody is saying something."

Rosemary was annoying, but listening to Clarice chatter on and on all morning about Tony saying this and Tony saying that drove Eleanor completely insane.

"And I actually *talked* to Tony the whole time. Me! We sat

on one of the picnic benches by Richardson's, and it was like we were best friends or something. He's going into the army, you know. He's waiting until they draft him. He wanted to be a Marine like Michael Williams, but they wouldn't take him. He can't see too well out of one eye." Clarice sighed, as if being half-blind made Tony the greatest hero on the block.

"That's too bad," Eleanor said. Back at the Academy, every time Sister Agnes wrote on the blackboard, the chalk screeched. The sound made Eleanor's teeth throb. Now Clarice's happiness made Eleanor's whole jaw throb.

"What about you, Eleanor?" Clarice asked. She picked at the buttons on her blouse. "Did you ever have someone that made you feel the way I do? Like the whole world is perfect and wonderful and nothing bad can ever happen?"

Eleanor bent over the prescription cards strewn across the desk, but her eyes focused on *Six Weeks!!!!!* "Robert," she said finally.

Clarice sounded flustered. "Robert? That's wonderful. I mean, I didn't know. You never mentioned him before. Is he . . ." Clarice struggled for the right words. "Is he still a friend?"

The second hand on clocks used to tick in rhythm with Eleanor's heartbeat. Daddy had said once, "I could set my watch by your heartbeat, sweetheart. Sixty beats a minute."

Now Eleanor's heart beat twice for every tick of the clock on the cubby wall. "Robert's a soldier." *Thump-thump, thump-thump.* "I've known him for a while."

Clarice sounded just like Lindy when Lindy had too much joy to contain. Or like Eleanor the way she used to be — the way she was when Daddy used to call her his Mouth Machine.

"That's so great! It's so great that you came to work here. I mean, Susan's my best friend and everything, and I used to feel a little shy about working when she wasn't here. But not anymore."

She lowered her voice. "I'm glad we're in *like* at the same time, too. That way I can tell you things I can't tell Susan. I don't talk very much about Tony around Susan. It would seem kind of mean, even though she doesn't like him anymore."

Clarice didn't know how lucky she was. She liked Tony. Tony liked her. End of story. Why couldn't love be that simple for Eleanor?

She covered most of a prescription card with her elbow, as if she were protecting a test paper from cheating eyes. She wrote *why, why, why* on every blank space on the card.

Clarice was still babbling. "But summer's already half over, and you and I are just getting to know each other. Before you know it, we'll be back in school, and we'll never see each other again. And I won't have anyone to talk to about Tony."

The word exploded into the air like a firecracker going off. "Why!"

Clarice tilted her head. Her hair fell across her cheek. Strands of hair brushed her lips and chin, and she pushed them back. "I don't understand. Why?"

The question kept echoing through Eleanor's head. Why can't love be simple? But Clarice would never understand. People who were happy in love wouldn't know. "Why do you want to be my friend?" Eleanor asked instead.

A perfect pink circle appeared on each of Clarice's cheeks. "Because." She didn't speak for a moment, but then her words tumbled all over each other. "Because you're smart. And brave. And I've never been either of those things before — not in my entire life. And I thought maybe if I could be friends with you, some of your smartness and bravery would rub off on me."

Eleanor couldn't see the cards on the desk anymore. She couldn't see Clarice, either. "After school — we'll see each other then," she mumbled. "And weekends, too. Mr. Carvelli asked me to fill in on Saturdays."

"Ma doesn't let me work during the school year."

Eleanor knew so little about Clarice — where she lived, whether she had brothers or sisters, what her parents were like. "We'll find a time. I promise."

Clarice rested her shoulder against the doorframe. "Can't you go to Washington Heights with me? We'd be together then. Eat lunch together. Maybe join the glee club together. There's so much to do at Washington Heights . . ."

"I want to write." Eleanor's chin quivered so hard that she had to tighten her jaw muscles in order to continue. "I want to make people feel things with my words."

"Well, then, Washington Heights would be just perfect for you. We have all kinds of art and music and writing classes. You'd love it so much! And we could talk about the war, and how scary it is to care about someone who's actually in it."

Eleanor's stomach turned over. She didn't want to think about fighting, or about war, or about boys dying.

She wanted to go to Mahoney's Point again, sit on the sea wall, and send her thoughts to Robert. All her longings and wishes and dreams. They would reach him. She knew that absolutely. Yesterday afternoon, in the cold drizzle, she had walked onto the beach and skipped stones across the surface of the water — one stone for each day that Robert would spend on the ocean. *Please, Robert. Please don't hate me. Please understand. Please write to me.*

He would. Of course he would. This was Robert, who loved his dog. And his parents. And her letters.

"Eleanor? Hey, Eleanor." Clarice tapped Eleanor's shoulder "I've got to get going. There's a counter full of people. But think about Washington Heights, okay? And all those classes. And me?"

She gave a tiny wave and disappeared into the store.

Eleanor waited until her throat felt drier than the Sahara Desert before she wandered out in search of something to drink.

Clarice stood at the counter, chopping an onion. *Whap. Whap. Whap.* She didn't look at the cutting board. Instead, her eyes stared at some spot on the back wall. Her mouth was frozen into a perfect straight line.

Rosemary stood behind the soda fountain. "You shoulda been here," she was telling Ed, the policeman. Ed had folded his arms across his chest, and the fingers on one hand tapped against his shirtsleeve. Rosemary didn't notice his impatience. She was too busy performing for her audience of one.

"I'm telling you. I'm gonna have to take a couple of days off to calm my nerves, because yesterday it was like all hell was breaking loose, the way Mrs. Williams went nutso." She clenched her fists and shook them in front of Ed's face. "She was screaming about me making her sick. Like *I'm* the one who took Michael away. I swear to God. I thought she was gonna grab me by the throat when she lit into me."

Eleanor erupted. Her tone could have shattered every glass on the shelves above the sink. "That's enough!"

Rosemary's eyes widened. "I'm just making conversation."

"That's not conversation. That's hateful. Gossiping about Mrs. Williams that way. Saying such mean things about her. You should be ashamed of yourself."

Rosemary winced at every word. *Good.* Because Eleanor didn't feel like editing her words today. "Maybe you're right after all. Maybe you *should* take a couple of days off. You could practice being charitable to people who are suffering."

Rosemary threw her apron on the counter. "I'll take a couple of days, all right. Maybe I'll take a week. Maybe I'll just quit!"

She flounced out the door.

Clarice grabbed Rosemary's apron from the counter, folded it, and placed it on a shelf above the sink. "Good riddance," she said.

Ed winked at Eleanor. "Good for you."

Mr. Carvelli didn't say a word when they crossed from Tremont Avenue onto Bell Street, but Eleanor could feel the waves of his concern. Finally, at the corner of Oak and Grove, he gripped her arm a little tighter, forcing her to stop before they reached the curb.

"You are not my bright shining Eleanor today," he said. "You are not oohing and aahing over the flowers in Mr.

Gallant's windowboxes. You never mentioned the big tiger cat
— Monster Cat, you always call him — sitting on the railing
outside Linder's Books and Antiques. Eleanor, you have not
been seeing these things for a while now."

Eleanor could only nod.

"Is it your friend, Robert? Did he make you unhappy?"

In her mind, she drew the picture of Robert, writing to her
the night before he shipped out to France. He must have
stopped and chewed on the tip of his pencil a million times as
he wrote. Letters like that were hard to write. She should
know. But he had trusted her.

"It's *me* making me unhappy," she said.

"Your Robert, is he a nice boy?"

"He is."

"Is he still in New York?"

"He's overseas now. In France."

Mr. Carvelli let out a long breath. "Well, we will say a
prayer for him tonight, Angela and me. He must be scared, so
far away from home. And we will say a prayer for you, too. So
you don't worry so much." He patted her arm awkwardly. "I
understand about sadness, Eleanor. I have seen enough in my
own life. You just nod every once in a while to tell me you are
okay." Eleanor forced her head forward in a stiff little bob.

Long after Lindy fell asleep, Eleanor stared into the
darkness. Robert was scared. He had told her that. And soon,
somewhere in France, he would open her letter and read it,
maybe by the light of a single match. Maybe he thought that
some word of hers would take his fear away. He would find

her fear instead. But maybe, if miracles ever happen in this world, his eyes would blur, not from the lack of light, but because he loved her. And he didn't want her to be afraid anymore.

She could almost feel the touch of his hand on her scarred cheek.

In the morning, Eleanor took the letter she had written from under her mattress. She hesitated for just a moment. Then she wrote *Love* in her best penmanship and signed the letter.

She addressed the envelope and placed an airmail stamp in the upper righthand corner. She heard Lindy talking a mile a minute to Mr. Partenope, so she raced down the stairs to catch him before he could disappear.

He had just turned onto the sidewalk when she pushed past Lindy. "Mr. Partenope!" she called.

He waited for her. He held out his hand and took the letter. "I'll make sure it gets where it's going," he said.

"Thank you, Mr. Partenope."

"It could be a while," he said. "Like I told you, it could be more than a month when he writes back."

When he writes back, not *if,* Eleanor thought. Sometimes you had to have a little faith. "Thank you, Mr. Partenope," Eleanor said again.

Mr. Partenope beamed. "You have yourself a good day, Eleanor."

Chapter Fifteen

❧ ❧

"Eleanor, we're supposed to meet Sister Rene at ten o'clock, so we can get you registered for school," Mama called from the kitchen. "Lindy's all ready. I'm all ready. But you haven't even had your breakfast yet."

Eleanor stood in her bedroom and inspected Holy Family's uniform hanging in her closet. "I'll be there in a minute," she called back. The gray skirt and white blouse would make her look as ordinary as a gull. And it didn't matter how carefully Mama had stitched the hem on the skirt or how precise the tucks Mrs. Carvelli took in the front of the blouse.

"You gotta let the boys think you got bosoms," Mrs. Carvelli had said, her mouth full of pins.

"Holy Family is a girls' school," Eleanor explained.

Mrs. Carvelli stretched the fabric more tightly across

Eleanor's chest. "You think you won't see some boys going and coming?"

But nothing helped. The uniform was just plain ugly.

Eleanor's life felt just plain ugly. Because it hadn't been six weeks, the way Mr. Partenope had said. By Monday morning — by the time she had to walk up Holy Family's front stairs and slip through the school's double doors with all the other gray gulls — it would be exactly seven weeks and two days since she had sent her pathetic letter to Robert.

Every day that she wasn't working, she had waited on the Carvellis' bottom step. And every day, Mr. Partenope's glance flickered from his shoes to the Carvellis' front door. His mouth stretched across his face like an elastic, but the elastic never reached his eyes. He spoke in short sentences about the weather, or the price of sugar. He never talked anymore about letters to soldiers or from soldiers.

Thank you very much, Robert. He could have helped her. She could have carried one of his letters around in her pocket that first day at school and run her fingers along the edge every time she needed to be strong. And at lunchtime, she could have thought about this wonderful Robert who filled his letters with his dreams and fears, who cared about *her* and not her scars.

Eleanor dug under her mattress and pulled out the unmailed letters she had written to Robert. There were three of them now. Bright, sunshiny letters all ready and waiting for Robert.

Dear Robert, How did you survive your first ocean cruise? . . .

Dear Robert, Congratulate me on the improvements in my

196

cooking. I made a hamburger for Ed, the policeman. He actually ate it and asked for another one . . .

Dear Robert, The good news is that Rosemary Myers was on vacation for a whole week. The bad news is that she was on vacation for only a week . . .

She flattened them, then scattered the pages over her bed until she had papered the bedspread with her writing. Then, one by one, she folded the letters and placed them back under the mattress.

Robert, Robert, Robert.

In the hospital, when Dr. Gilligan had removed her bandages and replaced them, stripping away skin each time he did so, making her cry from the pain, he had never hurt her one-millionth as much as Robert had hurt her.

Mama waited with Lindy by the kitchen door. Lindy wore a pink-checked dress Mrs. Carvelli had made, and she swirled on her toes like a ballerina the minute Eleanor walked into the room.

"I'm a princess!" she sang.

Mama wasn't singing. "You don't even have time to grab something to eat," she scolded.

"Why can't you do this without me?" Eleanor asked.

"Sister Rene wants to talk to you about your class schedule."

"I don't even know why I have to go to school, Mama. I have a job. I help with the bills, don't I?"

"Eleanor, you are much too intelligent to work at Carvelli's the rest of your life. It's fine for a summer job, but I won't allow you to waste your mind like that."

Lindy stopped mid-twirl. "Are you fighting?" She crushed the folds of her dress. "I get scared when you fight."

Mama's hand rested on Lindy's shoulder. "We're not fighting, sweetie. Eleanor and I are just discussing something. And the discussion is over." Her voice had that "you have no choice" sound to it. "I'm trying to do what your father would have wanted, Eleanor. And it's not always easy."

"If I could just go to Washington Heights with Clarice," Eleanor protested. "I know her. I know some of the other kids."

"You'll get to know the girls at Holy Family just as well. It will be a new school for you — a fresh start."

The subject was closed. So was Mama's mouth. Her heels clicked along Everett Street and then Ocean Avenue. Eleanor and Lindy had to scramble to keep up. "Watch your step," Mama told them as they climbed into the streetcar at the corner of Ocean and Ash. It was the last thing she said until they reached the convent steps.

Before she pressed the doorbell, Mama pulled out her handkerchief, touched her tongue to it, and wiped a spot of dirt off Lindy's face.

"Ooh, Mama," Lindy complained.

"Hush now."

Mama's eyes bored into Eleanor's face. "Be polite," Mama said. "Don't tell Sister Rene we haven't been to church for a while. It's high time we started again. It's just that we've been through so many changes lately. But that's our business. Sister Rene doesn't need to know that."

Sister Rene also didn't need to know that Eleanor and Marybeth had been kicked out for giggling the last time Eleanor had set foot inside a church. It had happened on a Saturday afternoon. They sat at the end of a row of elderly women who wore black mantillas and draped rosary beads over their hands. Most of them looked holier than the saints listed in Eleanor's missal. The women moved their mouths when they prayed. What possible sins could old ladies have committed? When Eleanor asked Marybeth the question, Marybeth sprayed spit all over the bench in front of them.

"Sins of the flesh," Marybeth said.

Eleanor burst out laughing.

Father Berube burst out of the confessional. "Go!" he bellowed.

Eleanor and Marybeth went. They hurried through the chapel door. The minute they reached the sidewalk, they laughed so loudly that passersby crossed to the other side of the street. "I don't think I can breathe anymore," Marybeth said between gasps.

"Dead. We'll be *dead*." Eleanor grabbed the light pole to keep from collapsing. "Our tombstones will say, 'Died from sins of the flesh.'"

Sister Rene Edward would not have laughed about "sins of the flesh." She stood almost a foot taller than Eleanor, and even under her white, starched bib, Eleanor could see shoulders wider than most men had. Eleanor and her friends at the Academy would have named her "The General." Her eyes lingered for a moment on Eleanor's face. Then they checked the length of Eleanor's skirt. "We've been expecting you," she said pointedly, examining the watch hanging from her waist.

She led them into one of the visitors' rooms. Eleanor expected to see pictures of Mary and Joseph and half the saints who ever lived. But the walls were bare except for a crucifix. It hung on the opposite wall above a small fireplace.

"Please sit down," Sister Rene said, pointing to three armchairs facing the fireplace. "I'll be back in a moment."

Mama and Lindy and Eleanor sat. They folded their hands on their laps. Mama and Eleanor's feet were planted firmly on the floor. "I feel as if I am starting school all over again," Mama whispered.

"Is she the boss of the nuns?" Lindy asked.

"I'm the principal of the school," Sister Rene said from the doorway behind them.

Sister Rene was carrying a tray that held three glasses filled with chocolate milk and a plate of Twinkies.

Eleanor couldn't tell who jumped higher, her or Mama. But Lindy was ecstatic. "Twinkies! Nuns eat Twinkies?"

Sister Rene must have answered Lindy. And Eleanor knew absolutely that Mama and Sister Rene must have discussed Eleanor's class schedule for the fall, because suddenly Eleanor held a list of classes in her hand. But the minute she saw those Twinkies, a tornado could have blown through the visitor's room and Eleanor wouldn't have noticed. She was too busy planning what she would write to Robert in her next letter. *Sister Rene fed us chocolate milk and Twinkies. Can you believe a convent actually has Twinkies in its cupboards?*

I have this vision of some nun with a late-night hunger attack rummaging through the kitchen, searching for them.

"So what do you think?" Sister Rene asked.

Eleanor looked up, startled. "I think . . ." What was she supposed to be thinking?

Mama rescued her. "Everything looks just fine, Sister. I think Eleanor and Lindy will be very happy here at Holy Family. And thank you very much." Mama nudged Eleanor's ribs.

"Yes, of course. Sister, thank you." She glanced at the schedule in her hand: Physics, Latin 3, French 4, U.S. History, and English 4. "Isn't there a class in writing I could take? I like to write."

Sister Rene's shoulders twitched. "I think you'll be just fine in English 4, Eleanor. We are stretching the rules as it is, by allowing you to graduate next June. After all, you did miss a good part of last year. Creative Writing is a rigorous class. We don't want to burden you with too much after all you've been through."

Burden. Sister Rene had no idea. The real burden was sitting through boring classes that Eleanor didn't care about. Having to pretend that she was grateful to Sister — was a burden, too. How could writing what was in her heart and mind ever be anything but a joy?

But Mama didn't hear the word "burden" the way Eleanor did. Mama stood and shook Sister's hand. "Thank you for all your help," she said. But she didn't make a move toward the door, even though Eleanor had already walked over and placed her hand on the doorknob. Eleanor's toes tapped against the soles of her shoes.

"Wait until I tell Jeannie that nuns have Twinkies!" Lindy said.

For the first time, Sister Rene actually smiled. "Let's keep it our little secret, shall we? If it gets out, everyone will want to join the convent."

She escorted them to the front door. "We will see you all next week, then."

The door closed. Mama turned to Eleanor. "That wasn't so bad now, was it?" Her tone pleaded with Eleanor. "She seems very nice. Businesslike, the way nuns in charge always are. But she's very concerned about your welfare. And I think she's right about not burdening you with too much work."

Eleanor took Lindy's hand as they headed toward the streetcar stop. She ignored the zillions of questions Lindy asked. At the corner, she stood with her back toward Mama. Otherwise, she would have unleashed the words that pounded inside her head. *I have the same brain I had before the fire, Mama. I'm exactly the same person inside. I'm still Eleanor.*

Mama stopped at the Carvellis' apartment door. "We're going to check with Angela about Lindy's jumper," she said. One hand rested on Lindy's shoulder. "She's taking in the sides for me. I ordered a size six from the uniform company, but the armholes droop halfway to Lindy's waist." She laid the back of her other hand against Eleanor's cheek. "Are you all right? Do you want me to fix you something to eat?" Her touch was as tender as a butterfly's wings.

Eleanor pulled her cheek away from that touch. "I'm fine, Mama. I'll make a sandwich or something upstairs."

She headed straight for her bedroom. She took the paper and Daddy's fountain pen from the top drawer of her bureau. Her fingers slid down the barrel of the pen until they curled, crablike, at the tip.

September 7, 1944

Dear Robert,

We start school September 10. I'm dreading the first day. It feels sometimes as if I am always having to meet people and explain my face to them, when what I most want is to be safe with the people who know and love me for who I am.

You know what, Robert? Since the fire, I thought the only thing people would ever see was my scars. That's all some people ever see. But they're not everyone. When Mr. Carvelli notices me wearing a new dress, he says, "You look beautiful, Eleanor." I used to think he was just being nice. But he means it! And my friend, Clarice? She always tells me how much she admires me. She thinks I'm brave. Not brave physically, but brave enough to stand up for people, and brave enough to say what's on my mind.

I haven't been very brave where you are concerned.

I really loved you, Robert. But I was afraid to tell you. I was afraid you would be disgusted at the thought of being loved by someone who looks like me. But shouldn't being loved by somebody be an honor, at least as important as any medal anyone could give you?

I do want to tell you about something you've given to me.

*Your letters made me feel very special at a time when I needed
to feel that way. I will always be grateful to you for that.*
    Please do stay safe.

Love,
Eleanor P. Driscoll

She folded the pages inside an envelope and addressed the
front. Then she shoved it under her mattress. Someday, when
the shards of pain stopped slicing her heart into pieces, maybe
she would mail it.

She took the box of Robert's letters with her to the Point,
and sat on the sea wall. She didn't even bother to check for
invaders. Since Labor Day, only old men had walked along
the edges of the sea. She didn't have to hide her face from old
men. They smiled at her and tipped their hats. Just yesterday,
one of them had spoken to her. "You have beautiful eyes," he
said. "They remind me of my mother's eyes."

The words felt like Robert's hand on Eleanor's cheek. And
her "beautiful" eyes couldn't quite contain her gratitude.

The beach roses had faded. Most of the petals had already
scattered onto the wall and the sand beneath. Soon the
bushes would resemble the fingers of those old men.

It was time to say good-bye. One by one, she took
Robert's letters from the box. She wanted to crumple each
one, throw it into the ocean, and watch the tide carry Robert
away. But she couldn't even let go of the first page of the
very first letter he had written — the one that began *Dear
Eleanor, My name is Robert Bettencourt, and I am the*

soldier that received your letter. Seven weeks. She had been suffocating for too long.

Eleanor could see the redness when she pushed her thumb against the skin on her arm. She should really go home. It must be getting late. Mama would think enemy spies had kidnapped her.

Eleanor turned the corner onto Everett Street. She almost walked smack into Mr. Partenope, who was closing the Beauchamps' front gate.

Mr. Partenope didn't inspect his shoes this afternoon. Instead he grinned as he heaved his bulging sack over his shoulder. "Hey, Eleanor. How you doing?"

Mr. Partenope wasn't exactly the person Eleanor wanted to see right now. "Nice to see you, Mr. Partenope," she said, shifting the box of letters from her hands to under her arm. She tried to walk past Mr. Partenope, but he wasn't finished talking. "Just saw your sister playing with that doll of hers. She's something, she is."

"I'd like to stay and talk, but Mama's expecting me."

"Sure. I understand, but like I was saying, your sister — she's really something. The minute she sees me, she says, 'Oh, oh. I forgot. I have something for you. It's my good deed for the day.'"

Daddy used to tease Mama when one of her friends stayed beyond suppertime. "Should we give her the old 'Here's your hat, what's your hurry?' routine?" he would ask.

Mama's cheeks would redden. "Don't you dare!" But she could never quite hide the smile that played on her lips.

"That Lindy," Mr. Partenope was saying. "She disappears inside the house and comes back with a bunch of letters. I thought she was maybe getting me a drink of lemonade or something. But no, she hands me these letters, like I said. 'For Eleanor,' she says. 'Cause she's been through a lot and I'm gonna be her helper.'"

Letters? For Eleanor? "You mean she mailed letters to me?"

"Naw. She was mailing letters *for* you."

Eleanor tightened her hold on the box.

"Airmail letters? To a Robert Bettencourt?"

"To that soldier? Yeah. I even gave her the stamps for them. I showed her how to put them in the mailbox, too. So she would know how the next time. That's what you're supposed to do with kids. Don't do things for them, let them learn by doing."

"Mr. Partenope." The rest of the words froze in Eleanor's mouth, and she had to begin three times before she could actually get them out. "Mr. Partenope, is there any way to get those letters back?"

"Nope. They're the property of the good old USA now. 'Off we go into the wild blue yonder . . .'" Mr. Partenope sang. "You don't have to worry none, Eleanor. I told you, they're all stamped airmail. They'll be heading for New York tonight and then on to France tomorrow — "

Eleanor didn't wait to hear him finish the sentence.

The whole way down Everett Street, her heart hammered out the all those steps she had counted a lifetime ago. She kept saying little prayers that she didn't finish. *Oh God, please . . . If You just make it not true . . .*

Lindy sat on the front porch next to Mama.

Eleanor pushed her face right into Lindy's. "What did you do with my letters?"

Lindy's voice sounded tiny and scared. "I mailed them for you, Ellie. You kept forgetting, so I brought them to Mr. Partenope. He said I could put them in the box with all the other letters. He said they would get to Robert!"

"You took my letters?"

"They were under your mattress. You always put stuff under your mattress."

"You actually *mailed* my letters?" Eleanor dropped onto the step as if she had been shot. "Who told you to do that, Lindy?"

"I was being your helper. But it's all right, Eleanor. Mr. Partenope gave me the stamps, and I put them in the mailbox and everything."

Robert would receive all those letters. All those letters from this pathetic creature with the melted-wax face who wrote *Love* at the end of each one.

"Sweetie. It's not a disaster," Mama said. "There's no need to get upset. Robert will just receive them in a clump instead of one at a time."

"I'm not supposed to get upset? Mama. Those letters weren't supposed to be mailed. Not at all. Not ever!" Eleanor turned back toward Lindy. "They were my letters. My property. You had no right to touch things that belong to me."

"Don't talk to your sister that way, Eleanor. She made a mistake, that's all."

Lindy was crying harder than Eleanor had ever seen her cry before. "I was just trying to help," she wailed.

Eleanor mimicked Lindy's tone. "I was just trying to help."
Lindy cringed against Mama.

"That's enough!" Mama's voice had never been as sharp.

Eleanor's voice had never been as shrill. "She's always
taking my things, always sticking her nose in where it doesn't
belong. But you never say, 'That's enough!' to her. It's okay if
she ruins my life. It's okay if Robert reads things I never
wanted him to know. Whatever Lindy does is okay."

Lindy was repeating "I'm sorry," over and over in a shaky
voice. Eleanor shut her ears. "Lindy needs me to watch her
while you work. Then I get a job, because Lindy needs you
home more. Lindy needs everything. What about me? I need
things, too."

"Eleanor, I give the two of you everything I possibly can."
Mama's eyes were huge, and her eyelashes glittered.

"You don't know what I need, Mama. I need someone to
explain. Why people can't see me! I'm still Eleanor inside. I
still have Eleanor's feelings. Nothing has changed."

Mama touched Eleanor's shoulder. "Sweetie, please."

"Why, Mama? Because ugly people shouldn't get upset?
Because we're not supposed to have feelings?"

"Eleanor! Stop it. Now!"

But Eleanor couldn't stop. "'Eleanor's so strong. Eleanor's
so brave.' I don't want to be strong, Mama. I don't want to be
brave. I want my *face* back. I want to be me again, Mama.
Why can't I be me again?" She tore at her face, at her cheek
and her chin. Mama grabbed her hands and tried to hold onto
them, but Eleanor kept tearing away, ripping her skin until it
was raw and bleeding. "Daddy!" she cried. "He did this to me.

If he had only left me there, I could have died, like he did. Because I died anyway, Mama. Look at me! I died as surely as Daddy did."

She stopped clawing at her scars. Her hands slid to her lap. She felt as if she were watching a movie starring somebody else.

Mama's arm hugged her close. "Eleanor, Daddy didn't mean to hurt you. He saved your life. Oh, honey, I know you believe that. This is all because of some letters? Sweetie, did Robert say something to you? Or write something? Did he hurt you somehow? Tell me what's wrong. Please, Eleanor."

I'll tell you what's wrong, Mama. You were right. You were absolutely right when you said Robert would get the wrong idea. He did. He thought I was a completely different Eleanor, and he doesn't care about this one. And now he'll read those letters and be even more disgusted. That's what's wrong, Mama.

But Eleanor couldn't tell Mama the truth. She couldn't tell *anybody* that. She stood on shaking legs, then pulled away when Mama tried to hold her back. "No, Mama. Nobody did anything. This is just me. It's always just me."

She turned and walked down the steps and through the front gate. Mama called her name again and again, but Eleanor kept walking.

Chapter Sixteen

$\mathcal{S}$ $\mathcal{S}$

Eleanor stood on top of the sea wall. Her eyes were filled with the ocean. The water shimmered in the sunlight, creating ribbons of silver rippling through blue sea. *This is the gift I wanted to give you, Robert. This ocean, all wrapped up like a birthday present.*

She picked up a flat rock and skipped it across the surface of the water. *Why couldn't you just write to me?* The rock bounced twice and disappeared without a splash. She picked up another rock and another. She threw them both as far as she could. *Why? Why?*

Suddenly, she was scraping the wall with her fingernails, freeing pebbles from the cement and flinging them in front of her, handfuls at a time. *I'm me. I'm still me. Other people see that. Why don't you?*

But the ocean wasn't angry enough today. The waves didn't punish the shore enough. So she walked instead.

In the saddle shoes that pinched her toes, Eleanor walked down Ocean Avenue and across Galvin Boulevard. People waited in line for the Tornado, and Eleanor pushed past them. Her shoulder brushed against one boy. "Hey! Watch it!" he called out. Eleanor turned toward him for a moment. "Sorry," he muttered.

"No. I'm the one who's sorry," she said.

She walked the length of Tremont Avenue, past the window of Byrd's Bakery, past Porzio's Insurance Company, until her breath came in great gulps, and she thought she would collapse. She would have kept walking, too, kept trying to find a safe place, except — in a flash of understanding — she knew where she had needed to go all along.

No people talking in hushed tones crowded Mrs. Williams's front stairs. No light shone through the dusk. On the bay window, the points of a gold star curled away from the glass.

Eleanor knocked on the door and waited. From inside, she heard the muffled sound of a chair scraping the floor, but no one came to the door. She waited for what she hoped was the proper amount of time and knocked again. No one answered.

"Mrs. Williams? It's me, Eleanor," she called.

She heard the scraping sound again, and this time the porch light flickered on as the door opened — just a crack at first, then wider.

"Eleanor. What on earth . . ." Mrs. Williams said.

But this was not Mrs. Williams. This was some stranger with Mrs. Williams's face and voice. Gone was the neat bun at the back of her head. Gone were the carefully pressed clothes, the warm eyes, the determined mouth.

"Eleanor?" the woman said again.

"I came . . . to see how you were doing."

Just for a moment, Mrs. Williams was back — sturdy, kind, and comforting. "Are you all right, honey?" she asked. But she didn't wait for an answer. She sighed deeply. "I'm not doing so well myself."

Mrs. Williams led Eleanor into the living room. Michael's picture still sat on the easel in front of the bay window. On the polished cherry table next to it, a vase held pink roses.

Elsewhere, newspapers and magazines, dirty cups and saucers littered every piece of furniture. Grains of sugar from an open bowl dusted the top of the coffee table. An afghan, once blue and white but now shades of gray, hung like a tablecloth over the radio console in one corner of the room.

Eleanor tried to clear off one end of the couch without fussing too much with the newspapers piled on top of it. Mrs. Williams reached over and cleared it for her, shoving the papers onto the floor in a messy heap that slid to one side. "I was just having a cup of coffee myself. Want some?" Again, she didn't wait for an answer. She picked up two of the cups sitting on the coffee table and carried them into the kitchen.

A grandfather clock in the corner of the living room chimed the quarter hour. Six forty-five. Eleanor examined the walls, the furniture, the newspaper headlines — anything to avoid seeing Michael's picture. The clock chimed again before Mrs. Williams returned holding two cups. One she handed to Eleanor. The other she balanced in her hand while she pushed pillows and a crumpled afghan from the other end of the couch. The hot coffee splashed onto Mrs. Williams's hand as she sat, but she didn't flinch.

Eleanor leaned over and took Mrs. Williams's burned hand into her own. "Mrs. Williams, are you all right?"

"I don't know, Eleanor. If I could just let go. If I could just stop *thinking* all the time. There must be a way I can stop thinking about Michael and pick up the pieces, but I don't know how to do that." Mrs. Williams patted Eleanor's cheek. "I'm sorry, honey. You just asked the wrong question on the wrong day. Not that any day is the right one. Not anymore."

"Can I do anything for you?"

Mrs. Williams took a handkerchief from the pocket of her housecoat and blew into it. "I'll be all right. I just need time. You know how that is." She pulled a photo album from beneath the pile of magazines and newspapers on the coffee table. "I've been looking through this," she said. She scooted closer to Eleanor and laid the album across both their laps. "This is Michael at three months." She pointed to a picture of a chubby infant in a sailor suit.

"He really was a beautiful baby," Eleanor said.

"Oh. Just wait until I show you the picture of him in first grade, at the Christmas pageant. He was Joseph. That's a special honor, you know — playing the father of Jesus." She turned the pages slowly. "I know it's here somewhere." Her fingers became frantic, flipping pages forward and back. "Ah. There."

A sweet boy stared out at Eleanor. He wore a bed sheet on his head that drooped over one eye. She wanted to pat his soft cheek. She wanted to tell him how much his mother still loved him and needed him. How was Mrs. Williams ever going to let go of that little boy?

Eleanor examined the coffee cup in her hand. It looked just like Mama's china, with the same tiny pink flowers strewn across the bowl and the handle. But Mama's cups had gold rims, and they were still sitting in boxes on the back porch.

When she was Lindy's age, Eleanor had often lain awake late in the night and heard Mama and Daddy talking. Her bare toes slid along the polished hall floors and down the stairs, following the hum of their voices into the kitchen. Mama sat at one end of the table, one of her hands curled beneath her chin as she listened to Daddy, the other curled around the handle of one of those gold-rimmed cups. Daddy sat at the other end of the table. He looked like a clumsy giant every time he lifted the fragile cup to his lips.

"Who said you could invade our castle?" he growled when he spotted Eleanor lurking in the doorway. But he always placed the coffee cup carefully on the table and patted his lap. Eleanor bounced onto it. She leaned her head against his chest, promising herself that this time she would stay awake, this one time she would find out what secrets Mama and Daddy shared when they thought she was asleep. But too soon, the steadiness of Daddy's breathing and the rhythm of his heartbeat against her ear made it impossible to keep her eyes open.

Ever since the move, Mama had said, "I have to get into those boxes someday and put the good dishes away." But she never had. Eleanor thought Mama was trying to get on with her life, leaving behind memories of a time when good dishes were the only ones they ever used. But Mama hadn't been trying to forget. She was just trying to learn how to survive in a world without Daddy.

"It was a dance," Mrs. Williams was saying, resting her hand on a page of pictures. "The teacher made him dance with this cute little girl. He came home in tears and said, 'Elizabeth's a girl, Mama. I can't dance with a girl!'"

The shards were back, making Eleanor bleed again. Mrs. Williams was never going to make things whole again. Not for herself. Not for Eleanor. No one was ever going to be able to make things whole for either of them ever again. She looked down again at the cup of coffee in her hand. Not even Daddy could have made things whole. No one could put back the pieces that people ripped from her with their stares; no one could force Robert to see all of Eleanor, not just her face, but her heart and mind as well. Just like no one was ever going to fill that hole inside Mrs. Williams where Michael used to live.

But Eleanor at least had Mama and Lindy and even Mr. and Mrs. Carvelli.

My own safe harbors.

She stood, letting the photograph album fall into Mrs. Williams's lap. "Mrs. Williams, I need to be getting home now."

Mrs. Williams looked up with eyes that reminded Eleanor of a hurt child. "So soon?"

"I'll be back to visit. I promise. We miss you so much, Mrs. Williams. Clarice still forgets to count the change out correctly. And you know how Rosemary is."

Mrs. Williams smiled for a moment, then the shadows took over. "Maybe someday," she said.

They hugged. "You're a good girl, Eleanor. A good strong girl. Your mother must be so proud of you."

Mrs. Williams's cheek brushed against Eleanor's. It had that rose petal softness to it. Eleanor whispered, "Take care of yourself, Mrs. Williams. I really will come back soon."

The air was cool when Eleanor stepped outside, and she wore no sweater. She stood under the streetlight as car after car passed by. Her feet began to hurt. Her legs ached. She should be getting home. Mama would worry. And Lindy — well, Lindy couldn't help being helpful and friendly. Eleanor had been that way, too.

She checked her pockets for streetcar fare. Nothing. Maybe she would tell Robert that in her next letter. She could twist the words around so he would laugh when she wrote about having to walk home. And then he would tease her about having no money — probably warning her as well. "You need to be more careful, Eleanor. I wouldn't want anything to happen to my ocean girl." Because he *would* write. He had to write, even if it was just one more time.

She shook her head to clear her mind of Robert. *I'm not going to do this. I'm not going to be Mrs. Williams.*

"Where have you been, young lady?" Mama stood in the doorway, her fingers curled around the molding, knuckles white against the polished wood.

"I'm sorry, Mama."

"Do you know how worried I've been? Mr. Carvelli has been all over town looking for you. We have been frantic. Mrs. Carvelli is all set to call the police."

"I didn't mean to scare you."

Mama's whole face collapsed, and she tottered against the doorjamb.

"Oh, Mama." But Mama turned toward the kitchen. She reached out with both hands and grabbed for the table. Then she dropped into a chair, put her head on the table, and sobbed.

Eleanor sat in the chair next to Mama. Her own eyes burned with tears. She looked up once and saw Lindy standing in the doorway, her eyes wide and frightened. Eleanor put her finger to her mouth. "Not yet," she mouthed. Lindy stepped back.

"All these times," Mama said between gulps of air. "All these times, I've watched you hurt and hurt and hurt." Mama wiped her tears away with the heel of her hand. "And all this time, I worried. How much more can she take? How much more hurt can she bear without Daddy to help? This afternoon, I thought . . ." She grabbed Eleanor and hugged her so tightly that Eleanor was sure her bones would break.

"I'm all right, Mama. *Really*. You don't have to worry about me."

"Not worry about you? Oh, Eleanor. I have been frantic about you."

"I went to see Mrs. Williams."

Mama folded her hands in front of her chest. "I should have guessed that."

"She's not doing very well," Eleanor said. "I don't think she'll be back to the drugstore very soon. It's as if she died when Michael died."

"Poor woman."

"I have to tell you something, Mama. About school."

Mama's voice had that edge to it. "Sweetie, we're not having that discussion right now."

"I'm not talking about not going to school, Mama. I'm talking about not going to Holy Family. I want to go to Washington Heights with Clarice."

"But Daddy wanted you to go to Catholic schools. We talked about it many times."

"Daddy wanted me to be happy. And it's so hard, Mama, when people don't understand. Clarice and some of those kids from the high school that hung around the soda fountain all summer — they already know what I look like. I won't be some kind of freak show to be pitied. Besides, Washington Heights has classes in writing, and that's what I want to do — write. I'm a good writer, Mama. I know I am."

You should be a writer, Eleanor. You make people feel things with your writing. She tried to shut out the words, to shut *him* out, to push Robert into the shadows with Jack Carmody. But she knew that Robert was the person who had given her the courage to face those shadows.

"I need something to hang onto, Mama I need something to make me feel special."

Mama patted Eleanor's cheek. "Oh, sweetie. You don't have to be a writer to be somebody special." She sighed. "But . . . perhaps Daddy will understand."

She said it the way she used to say things when Daddy would arrive home from the hospital.

Your father will understand why there are no hot dogs left from supper. Lindy fed them to the dog next door because he looked too skinny.

Daddy will understand why Gram's crystal vase is now shattered on the hearth. Eleanor and Marybeth had been practicing the jitterbug and crashed into the mantelpiece.

Eleanor had to know. "Do you believe in Heaven, Mama?"

Mama closed her eyes for a moment. "I didn't for the longest time," she said. "But now — I don't know." Mama's voice was hoarse. "Sometimes I feel Daddy's presence so strongly."

Lindy's face reappeared in the doorway. "Is it morning yet?" She stretched her mouth so wide Eleanor could just about see her tonsils.

"Come here, you little girl, you," Mama said and patted her legs. Lindy raced across the kitchen and bounced onto Mama's lap. Then she reached out her hand. "Do you still love me, Ellie?"

"Of course I still love you. But there's no room on Mama's lap for both of us."

Mama pulled Eleanor close. "There's always room for you, sweetie," she said. She pressed her lips against Lindy's hair, but her smile was all for Eleanor. "You are my sunshine," she sang, and Lindy's sleepy voice picked up the tune. "My only sunshine . . ."

Suddenly Mama's hand flew to her mouth. "Sweetie, I'm sorry. I forgot completely! You have a letter. Mrs. Carvelli brought it up. It got mixed up with their mail. I left it on your bed."

Eleanor pulled out of Mama's grasp. *Robert!*

"Sweetie, wait . . ." But Eleanor couldn't wait. Suddenly she was a bird, soaring a thousand feet in the air. She was a balloon, too light for her feet to touch the earth. She had known — she had always known. You can't love someone and not know how he feels about things. You can't trust someone that much and be disappointed.

*   *   *

There was a letter on the bed, all right. But it wasn't one of Robert's.

August 17, 1944

Dear Eleanor,

I am sorry to inform you that your friend Robert Bettencourt was killed last Friday morning while on patrol. He was checking out the forest perimeter to make sure it was safe for the rest of our squad when enemy shrapnel caught him in the back. He died instantly.

The other guys in the squad and me thought you should know how important you were to him. He was a pretty quiet guy, but when he did talk, it was all about you. It got to be a joke with us. "So, Robert, what would Eleanor say about all this?"

A couple of nights before he died, we were discussing home and what we'd do when we got there. Robert said the first thing he'd do is go to Massachusetts to teach Eleanor how to drive.

"If I don't teach her, she'll end up killing half the population of Beachmont and herself, too," he said. "If anything happens to me, I want somebody to teach Eleanor how to drive for me." I'm the one who said, "Sure, Robert. No problem."

So, Eleanor, if it's all right with you, when this war is over and things get back to normal, I'd like to keep that promise.

If you need anything or have any questions, you can write to me care of this address.

I have enclosed a scrap of paper I found in Robert's pocket when we were checking his belongings. He must have been writing a letter to you before he was killed.

Robert was a real good guy, Eleanor. And you were very special to him.

> *With my deepest regrets,*
> *PFC Guthrie Osborne*

The soldier's letter made no sense at first. Eleanor had to read it three times before she understood the words. Then coldness filled her body. No more letters? Not ever? No more *Robert, Robert, Robert.*

Eleanor had to sit on her bed. With her arms wrapped across her chest, she rocked and back and forth. Her hands squeezed her elbows so tightly they should have hurt. But she couldn't feel the pain.

The letter was a mistake, of course. Otherwise, Eleanor would have to curl up into a tiny ball to keep from crumbling into dust. The army made lots of mistakes in wartime. Just last week, they told Mrs. Whatever-Her-Name-Was on the next block that her son was missing in action, when really he just ended up in the wrong country somehow. That's what Mrs. Carvelli had said. What was the woman's name? Mrs. Carvelli would know. Mrs. Carvelli knew everything on earth.

That's what this was — a mistake of some kind. Hadn't the letter gone to the wrong apartment? Even Mr. Partenope made mistakes.

Robert couldn't be dead. Not now. Not when he talked to his friend about her, not when he wanted to see her someday and be with her someday, even though he knew about her scars.

And she still had so much to tell him — every tidbit of information about everything and anything on earth, just so she could hold onto him for a while longer.

She hadn't even told him how she felt about him. That she'd fallen in love. *I love you, Robert.* She had never meant to do that. It just happened somewhere between the pages of his letters.

Please! I won't ever love you again if you will just BE again. If I can feel you touching my cheek. If you can write just one more word.

But she had the one more word. It was still in the envelope.

Eleanor removed the scrap of paper. Robert's words were written on a Hershey bar wrapper. She was so afraid that the tears dripping all over her hands would smudge his writing that she placed the wrapper on the bed beside her.

Dear Eleanor,

I haven't been looking up at the stars lately. I was afraid that I would find you there. Then I realized you were the reason I noticed them in the first place. So tonight, if

But he had crossed out the *if* and written *when* instead.

Robert's words ended there.

Eleanor touched her smooth cheek. Then she touched the scarred one. *I was afraid, too, Robert. Afraid of the truth.*

She would go to Mahoney's Point. She would look at the stars and feel his light shining on her. And she would say, "Nice to finally meet you, Robert. I am the *real* Eleanor P. Driscoll. And I cannot tell you how much I love you."

But she had to do something first. She took a piece of stationery and Daddy's fountain pen from her top bureau drawer.

September 7, 1944

Dear Guthrie Osborne,

Thank you for telling me about Robert. It must have been a hard letter for you to write. I want you to know how much I appreciate your kindness.

I hope you will visit Beachmont after the war is over. You don't have to teach me how to drive. Some promises are too dangerous to keep.

Robert was very special to me, too. That scrap of paper you sent means a great deal.

Please stay safe.

Yours truly,
Eleanor P. Driscoll